© 2016 Frédéric Beigbeder
Illustrations © Rafael Alterio
© 2016 Assouline Publishing
3 Park Avenue, 27th Floor
New York, NY 10016 USA
Tel.: 212-989-6769   Fax: 212-647-0005
www.assouline.com
ISBN: 9781614285540

Art director: Camille Dubois
Editor: Amy L. Slingerland
Printed in China.

This is a dramatization inspired by true events. Certain scenes, incidents, characterizations,
dialogue, and letters have been fictionalized for dramatic purposes.

FRÉDÉRIC BEIGBEDER

Translated from the French by Adam Biles

MANHATTAN'S BABE

For Oona—With Love and Squalor

Illustrations by
RAFAEL ALTERIO

ASSOULINE

As proudly as my cat Kokoschka
bringing a sparrow to the pillow—dislocated,
bloody, but still breathing—
I lay this book, as well as my hardened heart
at the feet[1] of Madame Lara Micheli.

1. Compact and arched.

"Are you going to Scarborough Fair

(War bellows blazing in scarlet battalions)

Parsley, sage, rosemary, and thyme

(Generals order their soldiers to kill)

Remember me to one who lives there

(And to fight for a cause they've long ago forgotten)

She once was a true love of mine."

Anonymous bard, Yorkshire, sixteenth century

(Antiwar lyrics, in brackets, added by Paul Simon

in 1966)

When Diana Vreeland was asked if her most extravagant memories were fact or fiction, she replied: "It's faction."

THIS IS "FACTION"

*W*hen Diana Vreeland was asked if her most extravagant memories were fact or fiction, she replied: "It's faction."

This book is pure faction. Everything in it is rigorously exact—the characters are real, the places exist (or existed), the events are authentic, and the dates can be cross-checked in biographies and history textbooks. The rest is made up and, for this sacrilege, I beg the children, grandchildren, and great-grandchildren of my heroes to pardon the intrusion.

As the characters in this book led very secretive lives, the role of the novelist only increases. However, I would like to solemnly declare that if this story happens not to be true, I would be extremely disappointed.

F.B.

*I*n the spring of 1980, visitors to Paley Park in New York City bore witness to a rather unusual scene. At around three o'clock in the afternoon, a long, black limousine parked in front of the public garden. The chauffeur opened the door for a passenger, about sixty years of age and wearing a white pantsuit and sunglasses, who climbed slowly from the car. She stood still for a moment, nervously fingering her pearl necklace as if it were a rosary and she was at prayer, then made her way to the back of the park. Slowly approaching the waterfall, beneath the small trees, the rich lady took several pieces of broken china from her purse, after which her behavior became very strange indeed. She kneeled on the ground and began frantically digging at the soil with her manicured nails. A man eating a hot dog looked on, wondering why this bag lady was rummaging for food in the flowerbeds instead of in the trash cans at the other end of the square. At the time he didn't really pay her any mind, but it seemed that the woman, on all fours beneath the hanging garden, was burying her pieces of broken china in a hole and tamping down a clod of earth on top of them, like a child playing in a sandbox. Those who were finishing their lunch outside were even more astonished when the well-to-do lady stood up, her hands covered in soil, and climbed, with dignity, back into her Cadillac. Despite her sunglasses, they could discern on her face the satisfaction of a job well done. She looked just like another one of those eccentrics often

seen on the streets of New York—particularly since anti-depressants had become more readily available. The chauffeur closed the door again, walked around the car, climbed into the driver's seat, and the long sedan slid quietly toward Fifth Avenue.

JERRY:
AN INTRODUCTION

"I want to tell a story.
Will I ever know how to tell any story
other than my own?"

Pierre Drieu La Rochelle, *État Civil*, 1921

At the beginning of the twenty-tens, I realized that I no longer saw anybody my own age. I was surrounded by people who were twenty or thirty years younger than me. My girlfriend was born the year of my first wedding. Where had people from my generation gone?

Their disappearance had been progressive. The majority were busy with their work and their children. One day, they had just stopped leaving their offices and their homes. As I moved and changed my telephone number often, my old friends were unable to reach me. From time to time, when one of them died, I couldn't help thinking that these two tragedies might be related—when I'm no longer part of your life, life itself stops.

The dearth of contemporaries in my social circle may have had another explanation: I was fleeing my own reflection. Women in their forties made me anxious, with their neuroses so similar to my own: jealousy of youth, a hardened heart, unsolvable physical hang-ups, the fear of soon becoming unfuckable, or of already being so. As for men my age, they just trotted out memories of old parties as they drank, ate, got fat, and lost their hair. And they complained endlessly about their wives, or lack thereof. At the midpoints of their lives, people spoke of nothing but money...particularly the writers.

I had become a genuine gerontophobe. I had invented a new kind of apartheid—I only felt good with people for whom I was old enough to be their father. The company of teenagers forced me to make an effort with my clothes and to adapt my language and cultural reference points. They woke me up, galvanized me, made me smile. To greet young people, I had to slide my palm over theirs, then bump fists before finally tapping the left side of my chest. A simple handshake would have betrayed the generational divide. I also had to avoid dated slang like "what's up, bro...". ("Is he for real?")

When I ran into old classmates, I didn't recognize them. I just smiled politely and escaped as quickly as I could. People of my own age were really too old for me. I carefully avoided dinners in town with married couples. I was frightened of middle-class obligations, particularly gatherings of forty-somethings in beige apartments with scented candles. What I had against people who knew me was precisely that: They knew me too well. I wanted to be a forty-five-year-old virgin. I only went out to new bars for shaggy-haired kids, or to slick, plastic nightclubs where the toilets held no memories, or to hip restaurants that my old partners in crime would only hear about two or three years later as they leafed through *Madame*

Figaro. Sometimes I would hit on a young girl who would end up explaining to me, with tender eyes, that her mother once went to the same debutante ball as me. My only concession to age was that I didn't tweet. I couldn't see the point in dispatching single sentences to strangers when they could all be gathered together in a book.

I realized that my refusal to associate with people my own age was a refusal to grow old. I confused adherence to the cult of youth with youth itself. In every wrinkle on the face of a loved one, we see our own death at work. I genuinely thought that if I spent time with teenagers who spoke about Robert Pattinson instead of Robert Redford that I would live longer. I was prejudiced against myself. You can play at Dorian Gray without having to hide an evil self-portrait in the attic. All you have to do is grow a beard so that you can't see your own face in the mirror, deejay occasionally with old vinyl, wear T-shirts baggy enough that nobody can make out your expanding gut, refuse to wear reading glasses (as if a man reading a book at arm's length looks any younger), play tennis in an anthracite American Apparel tracksuit with white piping, model for the Kooples, dance with underage surfer girls at the Blue Cargo in Ilbarritz, and wake up with a hangover every morning.

At the beginning of the twenty-tens, I knew every word of Rihanna's songs. Which is to say, my situation was worrisome.

Three years earlier, in a diner in Hanover, New Hampshire, I chanced upon this photo of an adorable dead woman.

Her name was Oona O'Neill. Notice her Gene Tierney haircut (parted at the side, open at the front), her sparkling teeth, and the prominent carotid on her neck, bursting with her confidence in existence. Just knowing that this girl lived can give one courage. This brunette child with tinted eyebrows, filling her lungs with pure air, seems to believe that anything is possible. And yet, her childhood...

She was two years old when her father left her mother and moved to Europe with his new wife. Oona wrote him heartbreaking postcards: "Daddy, I love you so much. Don't forget me!" He would only see her again eight years later.

In 1940, Oona O'Neill was in love with my favorite writer.

I discovered this photo when J.D. Salinger still had three years to live. Along with Jean-Marie Périer, I had gone to Cornish, New Hampshire, to film a documentary about him. The idea was as absurd as it was trite—paying a visit to the world's most misanthropic author had become a kind of tourist trip for thousands of his fans. In 1953, the author of *The Catcher in the Rye* had moved to a farm in the middle of the New England forest. He hadn't published anything since 1965, the year I was born. He gave no interviews and refused all photographs and any contact with the outside world. As for me, I was the outside world, poised to invade his private realm with an HD camera. Why? Without really knowing it at the time, my attraction to this old genius had something to do with my growing disgust for people my own age. Salinger and I both liked much younger women. All his novels and short stories gave voice to children or teenagers. They symbolized lost innocence, unappreciated purity. Adults were ugly, stupid, boring, high-handed, caught up in their material comforts. His best short stories are those in which he uses childlike conversations to express his disgust

I chanced upon this photo of an adorable dead woman.
Her name was Oona O'Neill.

for materialism. Perhaps his philosophy was puerile. It was certainly false and possibly dangerous. But Salinger had invented the ideology of which I was a perpetual victim. He was the author who had best defined the modern world: a world divided into two camps. On one side, the serious people, the good tie-wearing citizens, the old bourgeois men with their offices and superficial housewives who play golf, read essays on economics, and accept the capitalist system just as it is. "Guys that always talk about how many miles they get to a gallon in their goddam cars." And on the other, immature adolescents, sad children forever stuck in the first year of high school. Rebels who dance all night and lunatics who roam through the forests. The ones who ask questions about the Central Park ducks, chat with hobos or nuns, fall in love with sixteen-year-old girls, and never work. The ones who remain free, poor, solitary, dirty, and unhappy.... In short, eternal rebels who believe they're fighting the consumerist model but who, in reality, have been pushing Western countries deeper and deeper into debt these last sixty years, and who have been sold billions of dollars of mass-market goods since the 1940s (records, novels, films, TV series, clothes, women's magazines, video clips, bubble gum, cigarettes, perfume, cabriolets, soda, liquor, drugs, all products promoted by arrogant, mainstream dropouts). I needed to stand face-to-face with the founder of the developed world's infantile dream. Salinger is the writer who disgusted human beings with aging.

We rented a small truck to wind around the green hills and arrived in Cornish on a glorious spring morning—11:30, Thursday, May 31, 2007. The sky was blue, but it was still rather cold in the sun. Cold suns are useless. It is a swindle to talk about spring when it is this cold and you are just a few steps away from Canada. Salinger's address had been easy to find online. Since the invention of GPS, nobody on our planet can hide. Right now, I'm going to give you the address, which, for sixty years, was one of the world's most closely guarded secrets. In Cornish, there's an old covered bridge that spans the Connecticut River. When you cross it from the direction of Windsor, the neighboring village, you feel like Clint Eastwood in *The Bridges of Madison County*. Then you turn left onto Wilson Road and drive a few hundred feet, until on your right you see a small cemetery with gray headstones behind a low white fence. Next, take a right onto Platt Road, which climbs the hill beside the overgrown and moss-covered cemetery. If you make the trip at night, you'll feel like you're in Michael Jackson's "Thriller" video. The Salingerian quest requires courage. A lot of would-be reporters have turned back on the approach to the abundant greenery of the summit. Somewhere, Bernanos speaks about a "liquid silence." Before May 31, 2007, I had no idea what he meant by this. Yet in that truck, with the director Jean-Marie Périer and producer Guillaume Rappeneau, our hearts were in our boots. Jean-Marie had form. For example, he had covered the 1972 Rolling Stones tour, which was anything but a walk in the park. And now he was looking at me with dismay, as if to say: "It was you who had this stupid idea, kiddo. Don't crumble on us now...."

The road shrank away, winding among ditches of grass in the middle of huge pines, old birches, centuries-old maples, and oaks. The light was softened by the black foliage. In

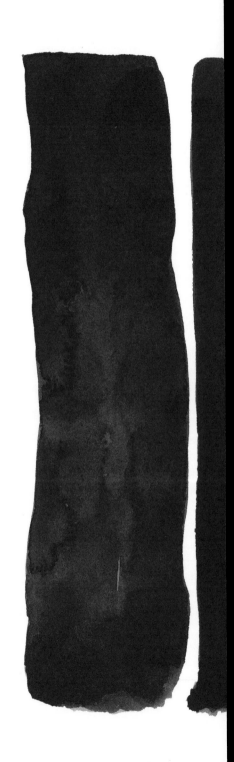

*The Salingerian quest requires courage.
A lot of would-be reporters have turned
back on the approach.*

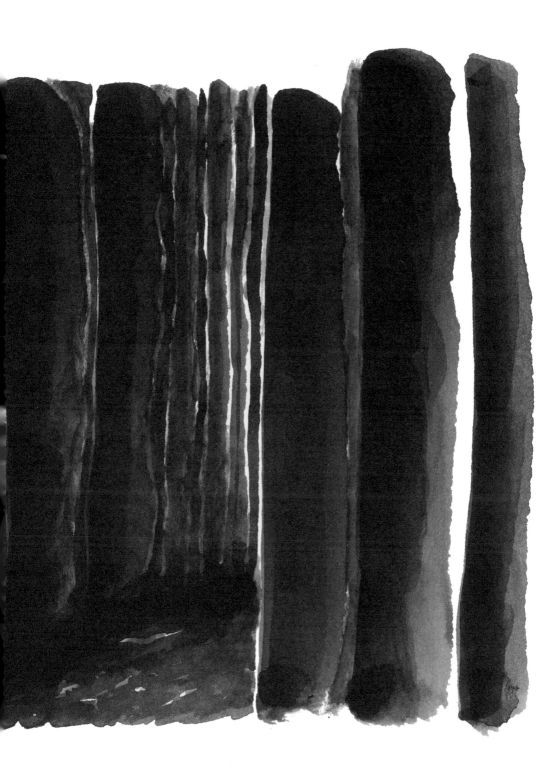

In Cornish, there's an old covered bridge that spans the Connecticut River.

this sepulchral forest, even in broad daylight, beneath the interlacing branches, it felt like midnight. Entering a forest is a magical rite: There are woodland traverses in every fairy tale, in German Romantic literature as much as in Walt Disney films. The sun was blinking through the trees: day, night, day, night. The light appeared and disappeared again as if the sun wanted to send us a message in Morse. "Turn back. Stop. Escape while you still can. Halt. Mayday. Mayday!" Romantic forests can quickly become hostile, as in *The Blair Witch Project* or at Hürtgen, during the hellish winter of 1944–1945. I knew I was going to chicken out. I would never dare disturb the man who had made me want to read, this American writer who was tenderness and rebellion personified. My mother had raised me well, and I was much too shy. Half a mile into the woods, there was a clearing on the right. Light came flooding back, as if God had turned on a giant spot. It was like a clearing, but when a clearing slopes, isn't it called a meadow, or a field, or a vale? What do I know? I grew up in a city. The track to J.D. Salinger's house is on Lang Road, the first on the right. It climbs, and there's a red barn to starboard. I can even give you his telephone number: 603-675-5244 (one of his biographers revealed it). It was there that I refused to get out of the car, there that I was trembling with fear, there that I was a coward. I imagined old man Salinger (eighty-eight at the time) meditating on a reclining chair, with his cats sharpening their claws on threadbare cushions on a veranda behind the house, beside a pile of logs. The cottage is on top of a hill. The view from his terrace must be marvelous, encompassing the river and the mottled prairies of white houses. The sky was streaked with brown birds, and the glacial sun illuminated the trees of Mount Ascutney, the blue mountain, opposite. The air was perfumed with sweet clover—I've looked up the names of the golden flowers strewn all over the county. Junipers covered the verdant hill, just like the ones in Sare that I liked to roll down, between the goats, when I was eight years old, covering my New Man trousers in cowpat. It was extremely quiet...like a panorama on the New World. Nobody on earth had the right to disturb a peace like this.

"Come on Fred," Guillaume said. "We didn't come all this way to turn back!"

"I... no... I didn't think that...." (Suddenly I had the same elocution as King George IV.) "I mean... we're not paparazzi...."

"Of course we are, you idiot. You work for *Voici*! Don't you understand? If he opens the door we'll have a global scoop. Even if he slams it in our faces, the photo will be seen around the world!"

"But... Salinger's in his eighties. He's as deaf as a post. And he's a World War II veteran. He's probably armed...."

"Ah. You could have told us that earlier."

In front of Salinger's farm, a wooden panel reads NO TRESPASSING. The day before, we had interviewed the novelist Stewart O'Nan in his garden a few miles from here. He had reminded me of the New Hampshire state slogan: "Live free or die." Automatic weapons were still freely available in this state, despite repeated school massacres.

"I knew you'd chicken out," Jean-Marie said. "You're a compulsive liar!"

"No, I... I'm... polite."

The cottage is on top of a hill. The view from his terrace must be marvelous.

The whole team burst out laughing inside the truck. I did too—out of politeness. But I wasn't fooling around. Courtesy, like shyness, is one of my great handicaps. I always thought that if everyone was as well-raised as I was, society wouldn't need laws. I just couldn't see myself ringing at the door of a recluse like a dirty kid dressed as a witch, demanding candy on Halloween.

Being a hermit is a respectable tradition in this region of the United States, ever since "the woman in white." From 1830 to 1886, the poet Emily Dickinson lived her whole reclusive life in Amherst, Massachusetts, an hour's drive south from Salinger's house. Dickinson, who would only be published after her death, wrote the following: "Absence is condensed presence." This sentence is about God, but also publicity. It isn't necessarily a choice to refuse society. It

is either a handicap, a social incapacity, or a calculation, a way of making yourself more present, forcing others to think about you; or it is to save your soul, to exist, to resonate. For Dickinson, it was without a doubt both sorrow and infirmity that kept her confined to her room. Certain of her biographers evoke a broken heart. She was in love with a reverend, a married father. An impossible love. Proust says the same thing as Emily Dickinson in *Pleasures and Days:* "Isn't absence, for someone who loves, the most certain, the most effective, the most long-lasting, the most indestructible, the most faithful of presences?"

This is where Oona O'Neill comes in. To excuse myself for having given up just a few feet from the goal, I took my team to lunch at Salinger's favorite restaurant, Lou's, in Hanover, next to Dartmouth University. The waitress wouldn't tell us the last time the writer had come there, though I read somewhere that he brunched there every Sunday. Everyone in the region respected the mythical author's tranquility. The radio was playing "Smoke Gets in Your Eyes," by the Platters. I was looking fixedly at a black-and-white photo on the wall, taken in a nightclub during the 1940s. Girls in evening dresses and pearl necklaces posing in the company of older men wearing three-piece suits and hats. Written on the frame: *Stork Club, 1940.* These fifty-somethings had undoubtedly died a long time ago, and the pretty girls smiling in the photo were either six feet under, or very close to being so, or drooling in wheelchairs with little or no memory of this joyous party. And then, beside it on the wall: Oona.

As I left the restaurant, I started shivering again. And yet spring was in the air. The yellow flowers hanging over the

Connecticut River are called goldenrod. Only old-timers take any interest in the names of flowers, and then only because they want to know what will soon be growing on top of them. In this region, there are fields of daisies so white they look like skiing pistes. Salinger's favorite writer, Francis Scott Fitzgerald, came to Dartmouth in February 1939 with Budd Schulberg to work on a screenplay called *Winter Carnival,* for

United Artists, the company founded by Charlie Chaplin. He was so drunk he had to be taken to a hospital in New York before being repatriated to Hollywood, where he died the following year while eating a bar of chocolate at Sheilah Graham's house at 1443 North Hayworth Avenue. Budd told me about his "work sessions" with Scott. I met him at the Deauville Film Festival in 2005, when he was awarded the literary prize. A few years before, in 1939, Salinger could well have gobbled down doughnuts in front of Dartmouth College with Miss O'Neill, Scott Fitzgerald, and Schulberg (Oona was fourteen, Salinger twenty, Scott forty-three, and Budd twenty-five). The older I get, the smaller my century looks.

I would have liked to have known if Salinger saw Oona again after the war. That's obviously the starry-eyed teen in me. I think it was Oona who inspired the Catcher that would forbid us forever from growing old. I will never know. Jerry Salinger died on January 27, 2010, three years after my aborted trip to his house. J.D. Salinger's letters to Oona O'Neill remain locked away in Corsier-sur-Vevey, Switzerland.

J.D. Salinger's letters to Oona O'Neill remain locked away
in Corsier-sur-Vevey, Switzerland.

Salinger's favorite restaurant, Lou's, in Hanover, next to Dartmouth University.

F. Scott Fitzgerald

Budd Schulberg

LOU'S

1
MANHATTAN
ROMANCE

"I knew he'd be a writer.
I could smell it."

Oona O'Neill on J.D. Salinger

*I*n New York, in 1940, everyone smoked. Everywhere. In bars, in restaurants, in taxis, in trains, and above all at the Stork Club. Leaving the club meant eyes that itched and hair that stank. People took less care of their health back then, because nobody nagged them about spiraling Medicare costs, Medicare not having been invented yet. It was almost eleven at night, and it was hard to make out the faces of patrons seated in the long barroom. The Stork wasn't a club; it was an opaque cloud. Under a net of party balloons, the tuxedoed orchestra covered Cab Calloway's numbers. Or, actually, was it Cab Calloway himself? Drawn on the wall, wearing a top hat and smoking his cigarette, was the eponymous stork. The restaurant was so crowded on Sunday nights that patrons had to shout out their drink orders to waiters in Spencer jackets and black bow ties. This didn't bother them, however: Americans always speak loudly, particularly when the bourbon's being poured generously over crushed ice.

In New York, in 1940, everyone
smoked. Everywhere. In bars,
in restaurants, in taxis, in trains,
and above all at the Stork Club.

The young man up from New Orleans, with blond hair and a high-pitched voice, could never stop himself from smiling when he was out with the Three Heiresses: Gloria Vanderbilt, Oona O'Neill, and Carol Marcus—the first it-girls in Western history, hidden behind a curtain of smoke. During the daytime, he sent his writing to magazines, which wouldn't publish it yet. And at night, he buffed his round glasses with a black silk handkerchief, perched them on his nose, and replaced the square of fabric in the left breast pocket of his white jacket, carefully leaving four triangles pointed at the ceiling, like arrows trained on the balloons hanging above his head. He thought that being well-dressed made you intelligent, and in his case, it was true. He was sixteen, his name was Truman Capote, and the scene took place at 3 East 53rd Street.

"My darlings! My swans!"

"What makes us your swans?" Gloria wondered, exhaling a gust of smoke in his face.

"Well, to begin with, you're white," Capote said, holding back a cough. "You carry yourselves elegantly. You have long, graceful necks..."

"And sharp orange beaks?"

"Indeed! You, Gloria, have a very sharp beak. You prove that every night. Except you smear it, and your teeth, with red lipstick."

"But where are our wings?" Oona asked.

Truman Capote only had eyes (blue) for the waiter, a young black man with gap teeth who looked like Jean-Michel Basquiat, long before the artist was born.

"Please be a darling and personally bring us four vodka

The Three Heiresses:
Oona O'Neill,
Gloria Vanderbilt,
and Carol Marcus—
the first it-girls in
Western history.

*The young man up from New Orleans, with blond hair
and a high-pitched voice, was Truman Capote.*

martinis. That way I know I'll get to see you again soon."

Truman smiled at the prettiest of the three girls.

"I broke your wings while you were sleeping, Oona darling," he said. "To stop you from flying away. I'm going to lock you all up for another decade yet. Don't worry, time will fly."

"Truman," Gloria said, "if we're your swans, what does that make you...a little piglet?"

They roared with laughter. Gloria had uttered this slight as if it settled the matter once and for all. Truman blushed. It's true that someone with a penchant for charcuterie would have found him hard to resist. Still, his blue eyes twinkled with mischief, and everything he said was light and amusing—quite unlike a plate of cold cuts.

In the same bar, on the other side of the room, a young man, six-foot-two-inches tall, was observing table six without saying a word. He never said a word. Anyway, all eyes in the Stork converged on table six, the corner table at the end of the L-shaped room. In 1940, Jerome David Salinger was twenty-one years old. He still lived with his parents at 1133 Park Avenue, on the corner of 91st Street. As he was tall, handsome, and well-dressed, he sometimes got let into the Stork Club alone, even though it was the most exclusive address in New York. His father was a Jew who had gotten rich off the back of kosher cheese and smoked meats. At that moment, Jerry had no reason to become the inventor of eternal adolescence.

At that moment, he was the tall, shy guy who lit his cigarettes with the same casualness as Humphrey Bogart—an impeccable gesture that had taken weeks in front of the bathroom mirror to perfect. Truman Capote is more of a snob,

Truman thought that being well-dressed made you intelligent,
and in his case, it was true.

but also more sensitive and amusing, and more full of himself as well. He is Salinger's physical opposite: small instead of a giant, eyes blue instead of black and piercing, hair blond instead of dark brown. One, the perfect little Alabama boy, the other a great oaf mimicking the New York intellectuals. They force themselves to chain-smoke so they don't look underage. They know how lucky they are to be drinking in this exclusive joint. It's the only moment in their lives when they have behaved like adults. Capote is already noting down everything he sees and repeating everything he hears. He knows full well that he would never be allowed in here without his three swans. They open doors for him. The red carpet is rolled out for them everywhere. They pose for photos in *Harper's Bazaar* and *Vogue.* They are postflappers and prefeminists. By partying and smoking and shimmying beneath strips of silk topped with glistening pearls, they are continuing, without realizing it, the slow emancipation that began in the 1920s and is far from being complete. He is just there to follow in their wake and to amuse these porcelain suffragettes. Thirty-five years later, he will write cruelly about them in *Answered Prayers,* his friends will turn their backs on him, and he will die heartbroken, pickled in alcohol, drugs, and sedatives. But for now, Truman wears the sweet little face of the child abandoned by his parents who learned early on that he had to accumulate memories to occupy his loneliness. Parties are never free for artists. Writers who go out at night never completely lose themselves. They're working. You think that they're fooling around, when in fact they're at their desks, looking for the sentence that will justify the hangover the following morning. If the harvest is good, a few words will survive the cut and be built into a paragraph. If the evening is a failure, there'll be nothing in stock, not even a metaphor, a joke, a pun, or a piece of gossip. Unfortunately, when there's nothing to glean, writers don't admit defeat. Failure provides a pretext for going out more, drinking more, like gold prospectors digging desperately in an abandoned mine.

J.D. Salinger approached their table. He always stooped a little so he didn't loom too much over other people. He wasn't only the tallest, but also the oldest. Under the table, Capote's foot wagged like the tail of an excited dog. He spoke first:

"*Mesdemoiselles,* who can tell me the species of this tall bird with black plumage? A heron, perhaps? A flamingo?"

"I'm Salinger. Jerry Salinger. Pleased to meet you. If we're talking birds, my favorite is..."—he thought about it a little too long—"the Short-Trousered American Chick."

Quite an achievement making the city's three most stuck-up girls smile. Truman got the message and watched as the beanpole stooped to kiss each of them on the hand. If he had been a bird, he would have been a stork...and so fit right in at the club. Oona was the shyest of them all. The sweetest, too, despite her strapless black dress. Her silence, her burnet flushes, her impenetrable dark eyes: She looked like one of Jean-Baptiste Greuze's ingénues. She didn't seem to know that she was beautiful, despite having been told so since her birth, by everyone except her father. Her awkwardness, her lack of self-confidence, the stuttering nature of her every move, her way of holding her glass close to her chest, of stirring the ice cubes with her index finger before sucking it as if it were bleeding, of always apologizing for being

They force themselves to chain-smoke so they don't look underage. They know how lucky they are to be drinking in this exclusive joint. It's the only moment in their lives when they have behaved like adults.

there as if she hadn't caught on that the club needed her if it wanted to stay fashionable. The adjective *clumsy* could have been invented to describe her formidable gaucherie. People wanted to adopt this stray cat. Gloria was more sophisticated, Carol was blonder—she copied Jean Harlow's finger waves and hand-drawn eyebrows. This was the secret of their friendship: They weren't just a trio, they were a range. One for every taste, nobody in competition with anyone else. For those who liked sophisticated women, vamps, femmes fatales, there was Gloria, the billionaire. For those who preferred more sensual or hysterical women, or those who were terrified of boredom or who enjoyed getting screamed at, Carol was the only choice. And for those not attracted to money or extravagance, for those looking for an autistic child to protect or an angel to save, Oona's trap was set.

Oona's calmness won her respect. She was the least exuberant of the gang, but not the least captivating. When she smiled, a pair of dimples tugged at her cheeks, and it was said that, deep down, her sparkling eyes made life almost bearable. Since Oona had turned fifteen, her mother had hardly bothered with her. She lived with Carol at 420 Park Avenue. Since she had turned fifteen, the blue-uniformed doorman let Oona O'Neill into the Stork whenever she wanted, because the owner was obsessed with her surname. Sherman Billingsley watched over her, called her "my most beautiful baby," kept the best table in the VIP Cub Room just for her, and picked up her check. He was as snobbish as a bidet in the Waldorf Astoria, and that was how he ran his business. A gang of pretty girls, even—indeed, *especially*—underage girls, livened things up, particularly if their famous surnames

Sherman Billingsley, owner of the Stork Club

attracted photographers and wealthy men.

"Move up, ladies," Truman said. "Make way for Jerry! Jerry, let me introduce my swans."

"This young lady doesn't really look like a swan. More like a wounded dove. What's your name, my little fallen nestling?"

"Err…" Oona hesitated. "You're going to razz me about it…."

"Tell me anyway."

"Oona. It's Gaelic."

"It's pretty, Oona. What does it mean?"

"*Unique.* So they say."

"Of course. How stupid I am! You can hear it. Oona. *One.*" Capote cackled.

"Una's a fairy in Celtic legend. The *queen* of the fairies," he said.

"Umm…and what are your magic powers?" Jerry asked.

At that moment, the young waiter brought their drinks. Also at that moment—I forgot to mention it earlier—Germany was occupying France. In Paris, allowing for the

*At that moment in Paris, allowing for the time difference,
German troops were parading down the Champs-Élysées.*

time difference, German troops were parading down the Champs-Élysées.

"So she does! Look," Truman replied. "Oona can make vodka appear on the table!"

"I can also make ashtrays vanish," Oona said.

"This kleptomaniac collects stolen ashtrays," Gloria sniggered.

"Makes you wonder what we pay the cops for," Carol said.

Oona smiled for the second time that evening. When Oona smiled, with her eyelids half closed, the din faded away. It was as if someone had turned the volume down on the rest of the world. That's how Jerry felt, anyway. Oona's mouth, the contrast between her red lips and white teeth, her high cheekbones, her claret nail varnish that matched her cherry-colored mouth.... This perfect high-society girl made him go completely deaf. What was it with this brunette? How could this girl he'd barely known five minutes give him butterflies? Couldn't someone have forbidden her from using that surprised-child look? He wanted to call the cops too. The state should ban women from using their eyelids so effectively. Jerry muttered to himself:

"An anti-Oona law..."

"Pardon? What did you say?"

"He's mumbling!"

"Ha ha ha! Oona claims another victim," Truman said. "Now you can form a club with Orson!"

Truman turned his head to a table at the other end of the L from where Orson Welles was eyeing them over the shoulder of a girl who looked like Dolores del Rio but was, in fact, Errol Flynn's wife, the French actress Lili Damita, whose

When Oona smiled, with her eyelids half closed, the din faded away.
It was as if someone had turned the volume down on the
rest of the world. That's how Jerry felt.

husband was away filming. (It was impossible for a nobody to sit at the table at the other end of the L.) Orson Welles kept shooting mysterious glances at the girls, particularly Oona, before turning away as soon as he felt his mistress would catch him. At the age of twenty-five, the famous radio host was trying out the approach of supreme indifference. This method doesn't work with shy girls who, on the contrary, have to be encouraged. Ignore a social climber, and she'll probably notice it. But snub a shy girl, and you're doing her a favor. And you'll never get to know her, above all, if you're famous yourself, which makes you twice as scary as any normal guy. Orson Welles turned back to Lili Damita, who was swallowing a mouthful of crêpes suzette in front of him. Jerry Salinger played it differently: He spoke very quietly, monotonously, in the hope the others at the table wouldn't hear him. He spoke to Oona as if they were alone in the world, and as a result they became so, a little, that evening.

"Oona O'Neill. Your name is alliterative, in fact. I reckon..." Jerry went on "...that your father chose your Christian name because of its similarity to his surname. It's a narcissistic choice."

"I wouldn't know. He hasn't spoken to me since I told a magazine I was shanty Irish. He thinks I'll turn out wrong. Until then, it's him that ain't right. Ever since he stopped drinking. The last time I saw him, his hands were trembling."

But the rest of the table had excellent hearing.

"Oona will turn out right, precisely because she started out wrong," Gloria said. "Like the rest of us!"

"I never knew my father, and hers died when she was eighteen months old," Carol said, pointing at Gloria.

"For my part," Truman said, "my mother abandoned me when I was two."

"I was also two," said Oona, "but it was my father who hot-tailed it."

"A toast to the Gold Orphans Club!" Gloria added, lifting her glass.

The three girls clinked glasses with Truman and Jerry, who was almost ashamed that his parents were still married. The sound their glasses made as they bumped is the exact same tinkle the triangle makes in the third movement of Gershwin's Concerto in F.

"A little respect, please," said Truman. "You do know you're speaking to the Stork's future Glamour Girl?"

"Oh no, please!" Oona bristled. "You're not going to bring that up...."

"Raise your glasses to the new Zelda!"

Oona blushed again, with anger this time. It infuriated her that she blushed whenever they harped on about this stupid story. Every year, the clients of the Stork Club elected a "Glamour Girl," and that year she was one of the finalists. She hadn't asked for any of it, and it was because of this nonsense that her father was no longer speaking to her. Must one really consider it an honor to be elected Miss Swanky Club? No. Must one refuse this title as if it was of little importance? Again, no. Such were the dilemmas facing rich, young New Yorkers in 1940, at the very same moment a red-and-white flag, with a black swastika, was flapping atop the Eiffel Tower.

"It's not that comparisons with Zelda Fitzgerald are insulting," Oona said. "It's just that the most interesting thing about her is her husband's books."

"Do you write, Jerry?" Carol said. "You've got a writer's mug.
I can spot a writer in a crowd of thousands."

"I raise my glass to Francis *Scotch* Fitzgerald!" said Truman.

"Do you write, Jerry?" Carol said. "You've got a writer's mug. I can spot a writer in a crowd of thousands. They're filthy egoists, frightfully intelligent... and to be avoided like the plague."

"Do you think he looks intellectual?" Gloria asked. "He doesn't say much, does he?"

Jerry was wishing that he'd never heard that name: Oona. It rang like a groan of pleasure—Ooo!—followed by a scream of release—Aaa! And between the two vowels, the consonant that evoked the moon. This name was as hypnotic as its owner. Jerry told himself that men would always be able to fall flat on their faces if there were women like her around to pick them back up again.

"I...I've never seen your father's plays," he said. "But I know that he's our greatest playwright."

"Not the greatest," Truman said. "The only! He was the first one to write about the poor. I don't know if it was such a good idea—all those depressing sailors, big-hearted prostitutes, suicidal dropouts. What a downer!"

"Since his Nobel, he's become a national treasure," Jerry corrected him.

He had no idea but wanted to make the girl happy by standing up for her father. He also couldn't stand gratuitous, socialite aggression. He found it more inspiring to be funny without insulting people...which meant he wasn't funny often.

"More than anything, he's a bad father," Oona concluded, exhaling her cigarette smoke toward the ceiling as if she were lying on an analyst's couch.

"The Irish are all drunkards," Truman said. "Find me an Irishman who doesn't drink!"

"Writers are allowed to drink," Carol said. "But for fathers it's not advised."

"I'd love to know his work," Jerry went on. "You see, my problem, Miss O'Neill, is that theaters make me uneasy. I always want to cough when you absolutely mustn't, and I always feel like I'm on the creakiest seat in the whole room.... I don't know why I'm never able to forget that I'm sitting in front of human beings who are paid to recite dialogue. And the actors pass on their stage fright to me. I'm dead scared that they'll forget their lines!"

"There's also the spit," Truman said. "At the theater it's best to avoid the front few rows, or at least to come with a good umbrella."

"Forgive me," Jerry said. "I bet you're fed up with people speaking to you about your father."

"It's not an easy name to have," Oona said. "I consider myself more of an orphan than anyone's daughter. It's strange being the orphan of somebody who's both alive and famous. Everyone speaks to me about him as if we're close, whereas I've only seen him three times in the past ten years."

Oona shut up, annoyed at having confided something so intimate to a stranger. Sensing her friend's embarrassment, Gloria came to her assistance, singing "*Hi-de-hi-de-hi-de-ho!*" The orchestra was playing "Minnie the Moocher" a little too loudly. The vibrations of the double bass were making the mahogany-covered walls tremble. The song tells the story of a prostitute looked after by a cokehead. It could have been the subject of one of Oona's father's plays. It's always amusing to see the middle classes singing violent lyrics in unison. At dinners with respectable families, in the presence of small children, I can't help smiling when everyone hums "Walk on the Wild Side" and mimics Lou Reed's *"Too too doo too doo too too doo doo"* unaware he's telling the story of a transvestite prostitute.

"Listen," Gloria Vanderbilt said. "So much the better that I inherited the family fortune. But I'd happily do away with all the rest: the photos, the gossip, the gigolos, the crooks.... What a mess! Truman, be a darling and order another round of vodka martinis."

Gloria's family built half of New York but demolished her childhood. While signaling to the maître d', Truman changed the subject. Whenever something painful came close, Truman ran the other way. It was a question of survival. That's what made him the most seductive teenager in New York.

"All these fatherless girls," he said to Jerry. "Somebody needs to look after them. They escaped from Park Avenue to study drama. All Upper East Side girls do theater because they all want to be loved, and the people who are supposed to love them have gone to the Hamptons for the weekend."

"My father's in Paris, and my mother's in Los Angeles," Oona said.

"Look at Orson over there," Carol said. "My God, he's sinister! Has he never acted in an O'Neill? He really should. I could easily see him beating his depressed wife with an empty bottle."

"I think he's almost handsome," Gloria said. "I loved it when his radio show made everyone believe the Martians were attacking Broadway."

"I don't know what was so sensational about that," Truman said. "The Martians attack 42nd Street every night."

Since eight o'clock that evening, Gloria Vanderbilt had been tossing *hellos* at every handsome guy who passed. If they smiled back at her, she left the table to go to the bar and came back with visiting cards that she'd show around the table before tossing them in the white ashtray. It was a great honor when the rich heiress remained seated on the red bench with her gang of noisy friends. Carol got up to dance with Truman. They were so blond! To pick them out among the other dancers, you only had to look for their glow in the middle of the dance floor, like two will-o'-the-wisps on a marsh.

To seduce a highly coveted girl, you have to make her believe you've got the time... even if you haven't. Don't throw yourself at her like the others, but show your interest all the same. It's a subtle and contradictory game. You have two minutes to get two messages across—"I couldn't give a damn" and "I *really* could...." In reality, if the girl stays with you longer than two minutes it means she has chosen you, in which case, just shut up.

Oona eyed Jerry discreetly as he bit his nails. She understood that he too was wondering what he was doing there. They were measuring each other up, without speaking. The mirror behind the bar had two uses: spying on others and checking your hairdo. From time to time, one of them opened their lips to start a sentence but couldn't. The other tried in turn, but nothing came out, save for a few scrolls of Chesterfield smoke. They were searching for something to say that wasn't banal. Each felt they had to be worthy of the other. That their conversation had to be deserved. Sometimes

they exchanged rumbling noises, but they spent most of this first half-hour encounter drinking tiny sips of vodka martini, carefully inspecting the bottom of their glasses as if seeking treasure, an olive, or simply composure.

"..."

"Err..."

"I..."

"..."

"Umm..."

"It's hot...."

"Yup..."

"..."

"This song..."

"'Smoke Gets in Your Eyes'?"

"Could be..."

"Mm..."

"..."

"..."

"Pretty title..."

"Yup..."

"Always got smoke in our eyes here...."

"Fred Astaire's version is the best. When he dances it looks like he's gliding...."

"Like a figure skater..."

"Mm... You know, you look a little like him."

"Oh?"

"..."

"Because of my long face?"

Uncomfortable smile.

Disconcerted sigh.

"Could you hand me the ashtray?"

"Here…"

"It's true my face is peanut-shaped."

"No! Fred Astaire is very handsome."

"I'm sorry to ask this but… how old are you?"

"Fifteen. Why?"

"…"

"…"

"No reason…"

"And you?"

"Twenty-one…"

"…"

"…"

"You know…"

"Yes?"

"I'm not saying much… but I'm not bored."

"Me neither."

"I like not saying much with you."

"…"

"…"

I'll stop transcribing the dialogue between these two now, because readers might either think I'm just stringing things out (which is true) or that I'm not giving them value for money (which is decidedly false). Yet it happens to be the exact transcription of the first nonconversation between Oona O'Neill and Jerome David Salinger. These two great paralytics didn't dare even look at each other, sitting side by side as they were, facing the room. They gazed at the waiters' ballet and listened to the orchestra belting out its tunes under the net of party balloons. Oona scratched at her napkin. Jerry sniffed

"When Fred Astaire dances it looks like he's gliding...."

at his glass as if he knew the slightest thing about martinis, his other hand clasping the armrest like someone terrified of flying at the moment of takeoff. Sometimes he raised one eyebrow. Sometimes two. The existence of "small talk" is well known. That night, Oona and Jerry invented "silent talk." A wordy silence, an emptiness full of allusions. The rest of the table was making noise over nothing. They exhibited a mute curiosity. It was irritating to see, so much and such sudden profundity in the middle of all of New York's frivolity. These two uneasy characters perhaps felt relieved to be able to finally shut up in unison. The others came back to sit down, exhausted by the dancing and the hunt. Truman looked tenderly at Jerry as he said things like:

"They say that Orson made a movie about the Hearst family. No newspaper will talk about it!"

"Stop devouring her with your gaze, darling. It's irritating. At least try to keep your mouth closed."

"Have you seen *The Great Dictator*? Chaplin is hilarious, but I found it strange to hear his voice. I thought it would be deeper."

"I love it when he speaks German," Carol said. "*Und Destretz Hedeflüten sagt den Flüten und destrutz Zett und sagt der Gefuhten*!!"

"And what does that mean?"

"Nothing! It's fake German. You really are bilingual when you drink."

"It could be that the real Hitler gives his speeches in kitchen-table German. That's why nobody believed what he was saying."

Carol, the blonde, laughed too loudly at her own jokes, in an attempt to shock them to life. She didn't like it when Oona got lucky. She didn't want to share her. She wanted to keep her all to herself, like the little sister she never had. It showed that she was annoyed because she took out her compact and started nervously tamping at her face with the powder puff. Gloria was happy not to be the only "daughter of" at the table. Such is the curse of celebrity daughters: Instead of taking advantage of their surnames with insouciance (after all, they didn't choose their parents), they always feel disfigured by them, like a handbag defaced by a chubby golden logo. But the three friends knew where they stood: Men were first and foremost attracted to their physical appearance. The fame and fortune of their parents was the (poisoned) icing on the cake of their willowy bodies. While they continued with their wisecracks, Jerry was frowning. It's not rocket science to guess what he was thinking: "But what is it that's so special about this girl? Why does her mousy head inspire me so? Why did I *instantly* adore her eyebrows and her sadness? Why do I feel so stupid and yet so good when I'm next to her? What am I waiting for? I should take her by the hand and carry her far away from here...."

"My favorite thing about Chaplin is Paulette Goddard," Gloria said. "Hell's bells, she's chic!"

"He has always had good taste in women. He picks them out very young," Truman murmured between his nonexistent lips.

"I didn't laugh at his *Dictator.* The European masses find little funny about Hitler." Jerry released this sentence then immediately regretted his inability to be lighthearted. "I wonder if he'd even seen it."

One second later, he stood up, turned toward the door, then turned back angrily to Oona, like an actor from the Royal Shakespeare Company exiting the stage:

"It was nice not talking with you, Miss O'Neill."

"Hey," Truman cried. "The night is still young!"

"I demand a crêpe suzette this instant," said Carol, "on pain of death!"

"Nice not to meet you too, Jerry," Oona said quietly. (Then, so as to hide her blushes, Oona turned toward her friends while the beanpole walked off toward the coat check,

"Have you seen The Great Dictator? *Chaplin is hilarious, but I found it strange to hear his voice. I thought it would be deeper."*

chewing on a piece of skin from his left thumb.) "What a peculiar oaf he is....What time is it, anyway?"

"Too early for bed," Truman said.

"We have to wait until they drop the balloons," Carol said.

"There's a great day coming mañana!" the band kicked in.

Every Sunday at the Stork Club was "Balloon Night." On the twelfth stroke of midnight, the girls fought to burst all the balloons that fell from above their heads. Inside some of them were vouchers for surprises, jewelry, presents, gifts, a dress, or a scarf.... The winners screamed even louder, on the point of orgasm, and the losers screamed too, with anger and jealousy, then everyone drowned these emotions in a flood of whiskey. This kind of "Balloon Night" should be brought back today. We lack those kind of explosive parties. As they burst, the hundreds of balloons sounded like a volley from an MP38 machine gun, briefly drowning out the rumba. Carol was the craziest of the trio. Standing on the table, she was ready to scratch or bite anybody who blocked her path toward the Prize Balloon, which she burst with fingernails filed into razors.[2]

J.D. Salinger walked back to his parents' place, not far from the building on Riverside Drive I lived in, forty-four years later, with my uncle George Harben. Oona's sad smile was etched into his memory and onto the Park Avenue facades. He examined his long face in shop windows. *Fucking Fred Astaire!* His head was cold because he had forgotten his hat at the Stork and was too ashamed to go back and pick it up in front of the whole gang. He would spend

---

2. Later, Carol had the reputation for being a real pain in the ass. Her last husband, the actor Walter Matthau, was the only person able to stand up to her. A famous anecdote: While constantly complaining about the cold during a freezing trip to Poland in the 1960s, during which they visited the memorial to a famous concentration camp, Matthau ended up

the next few weeks dissecting every second of that evening. Why did she sit with him for so long? Why couldn't he talk with her except through grunts? What should he have said to make himself unforgettable? As he reached his building and fumbled in his jacket pocket for his keys, he felt something heavy inside. Someone had slipped one of the Stork Club's white ashtrays into his jacket. Although inanimate, the vision of the smoking, top-hatted stork brought a smile back to his face.

telling her, "You ruined my trip to Auschwitz!" Gloria Vanderbilt was the hardest partier of the group. Orphaned at eighteen months old, she went on to marry four times, publish poems and erotic novels, and launch the first designer jeans. Later, she virtually invented the concept of the "cougar," and recounted intimate details of her love affairs in her memoirs.

2
THE NOBEL WINNER'S DAUGHTER

"Life is a fearing,
A long dying,
From birth to death!
God is a slayer!
Life is death!"

Eugene O'Neill, *Lazarus Laughed,* 1927

I n France, Eugene O'Neill has been somewhat forgotten. We neglect this surly, mustachioed playwright who imported Nordic realism to the United States. We prefer the originals to the copy: Ibsen (Norwegian) and Strindberg (Swedish) invented this theater of home life and metaphysical pains in the ass. In *A Doll's House* or *Miss Julie,* doors slam just as in the plays of Georges Feydeau, although we laugh much less when they do. Having read them all attentively, from 1917, Eugene O'Neill started putting on tortured dramas, adding alcohol, drugs, and whores to the mix for a little naturalist cachet. He chose his sets with care. The action took place on a whaling ship stuck in the Arctic ice, or in a grimy sailor's bar, or in a sanatorium for tuberculosis patients, or in the middle of a minefield.... All this hysterical folklore, the group psychoanalysis, the bitter monologues, today seem old-fashioned and pompous. Yet without Eugene O'Neill there would be no Tennessee Williams. And so no Marlon Brando. And so no Johnny Depp. Or Sean Penn. Or Ryan Gosling. You see, my young readers, the past is good for something.

Eugene O'Neill's life story is a tragedy. So obviously his art resembles it. If we list his misfortunes, we begin to forgive his laconic temperament. He was born in New York in 1888, just after the death of his two-year-old brother, Edmund, from a badly treated case of the measles. His mother, Ella O'Neill, would never get over this loss, becoming a morphine addict when Eugene was born. At the time, doctors readily prescribed hard drugs to young mothers to help them cope with the pain of childbirth. His father was an actor in Irish theater who drank to forget the death of his firstborn son, and who spent his life on tour, always playing the same role—Edmond Dantès in *The Count of Monte Cristo*. In *Long Day's Journey Into Night* (1942), Eugene O'Neill describes his battered mother who wanders about the house, her wedding dress in her hands, crying over the beautiful days past. It is a scene he witnessed often in his childhood. His mother's drug addiction made Eugene feel guilty. During his childhood, his father told him repeatedly that his mother started using the day after his birth. Eugene O'Neill tried to kill himself in 1912, at the age of 24. His brother Jamie succeeded, in November 1923. Eugene started drinking as much whiskey as his father. And then, one night in 1917, in New York, in the back room of a bar called Hell Hole, on the corner of

Eugene O'Neill's life story is a tragedy. So obviously his art resembles it.

One night in 1917, in New York, in the back room of a bar called Hell Hole, on the corner of Sixth Avenue and Fourth Street, Eugene saw Agnes Boulton.

FROM
JOHN SLOAN'S
"HELL HOLE"

Sixth Avenue and Fourth Street, he saw this person:

Agnes Boulton wanted to become a writer just like he did. While she waited, she wrote magazine articles and sometimes pulp fiction stories. Eugene started trembling with nerves. He was sitting in a corner of the bar staring at her sadly, like a frustrated lunatic. A mutual friend introduced them: "This is Gene O'Neill, the playwright." He continued eyeballing her, said nothing, and started drinking frantically, tracing concentric circles with the toe of his shoe in the sawdust on the floor. When Agnes wanted to leave the bar, Eugene offered to walk her back to the Brevoort, her Greenwich Village hotel. Intrigued by his mutism, she accepted. They walked silently through the night. When they arrived in front of the Brevoort, Agnes probably said something like, "OK, well, goodnight, then." She would never forget what Eugene O'Neill said next. Looking her right in the eye he said: "Agnes, I want to spend every night of my life from now on with you. I mean this. Every night of my life."

Agnes believed him. They got married within the year. Remember that sentence. It works with romantic, literary, or unbalanced young women. There's no point waiting to declare your love. With these crackpots you have to express your desire quickly, otherwise you just become an asexual boyfriend and it's ruined forever.

Eugene O'Neill didn't know it but—perhaps as a result of his childhood—he was allergic to fatherhood. When he learned that Agnes was pregnant, he went off to get drunk and didn't sober up at all during her pregnancy. Their daughter, Oona O'Neill, was born on May 14, 1925, in Bermuda. She had her mother's straight nose and her father's black eyes. Eugene thought she was very pretty but quickly decided that her bawling was messing with his writing. For Gene O'Neill, children were an obstacle to creation. They were a creation that stopped you from creating. Pregnant Agnes became a competitor, because he too was giving birth—to his work! "What's the good of bearing children? What's the use of giving birth to death?" he wrote in *The Great God Brown*. And there's also this monologue in *The First Man:* "Oh, damn all children!... Hatred! Yes, hatred! What's the use of denying it? I must tell someone.... I hate it. It!" Of course, these are theatrical characters and cannot be taken as expressing the author's personal opinion. That goes without saying.

Eugene O'Neill's other two sons (Eugene Jr., an alcoholic like his father, and Shane, a junkie like his grandmother) would later commit suicide. As long as Agnes only took care of him, Eugene was happy. From the moment his children were born, he dreamed of nothing but escape. Eugene, who during his childhood was neglected by an absent father and a mother who was detached from reality, would reproduce exactly the same pattern with his own children. It is not known if psychoanalysis cures neuroses, but here stands the

*When Agnes wanted to leave the bar, Eugene offered to walk her back to
the Brevoort, her Greenwich Village hotel.*

proof that the dramatic arts do not.

Welcome to Oona's family. The promise that Eugene made in front of the Brevoort wouldn't last long. Eugene O'Neill stopped seeing his children after he left Agnes for an actress when Oona was two years old. In 1928, he moved to Paris, where he remarried. However, he continued writing Oona to relieve him of the guilt of having abandoned her. The letters and photos that Eugene sent her from England, France, and China, in which he begged his little girl to remember him, can be considered as a modern, epistolary reworking of Tantalus's torture. Throughout her childhood and adolescence, Oona O'Neill only saw her father on three brief occasions. She loved him so much that she cried every time she saw him in the newspapers.

Eugene O'Neill's most famous play, *Long Day's Journey Into Night,* is so autobiographical that he demanded it only be published twenty-five years after his death. Carlotta, his widow, a bromide addict, didn't wait that long. The play was produced two years after Eugene's death, in 1956. In it, he exposed his familial nightmare: an aging and alcoholic father, a drug-addict mother, one son a failed actor, the other a tubercular sailor. He doesn't mention his daughter anywhere. "...alone with myself in another world... It was like walking on the bottom of the sea. As if I had drowned long ago. As if I was the ghost belonging to the fog..."

It is clear that happiness was not one of Eugene's gifts. Another of his texts, *The Rope* (1918), tells the story of a father who ties a noose around a beam in his barn, waiting for his son to hang himself.

People come from somewhere. The only masculine figure

in Oona O'Neill's life was a bad-tempered father, obsessed with the past, silence, secrets, and ghosts. A man whose favorite pastime was opening old wounds: "Life is a lie," he said. "Life is a solitary cell whose walls are mirrors." It's an expressive image, but its consequences are terrible. Eugene O'Neill was walled up by his own work. He could be friendly and kind one minute, then mean, cutting, and cruel the next. He fed upon his own despair. The pleasure of disappearing— it wasn't J.D. Salinger who invented it, but perhaps Eugene O'Neill, following on from Emily Dickinson. He was one of the first writers to describe a broken family, which would become the Western norm in the century that followed. He saw the end of the structure that Christian society had considered immutable. Anxiety, alcohol, solitude, and trauma are enormous advantages for a writer, but the greatest handicaps for a father. Maybe depressed writers should be forbidden from having children.

By dint of his imitation of Nordic writers, it was logical that Eugene O'Neill should be recognized by the Swedish. In 1936, the Nobel Prize for Literature was awarded to an illustrious contemporary playwright who had already received the Pulitzer three times in his own country, for *Beyond the Horizon, Anna Christie,* and *Strange Interlude.* (He would win a posthumous fourth for *Long Day's Journey Into Night.*)

During one of his rare visits to New York, Eugene O'Neill asked Oona to lunch with his new wife. After the meal, he took his children for a ride through Central Park in a large Cadillac. Oona was six. She threw up in the spanking-new car, all over her father and stepmother. Throughout the 1930s, she would try to make contact with this brilliant father whom everyone spoke about, but who never talked to her. Her numerous written requests for a visit, for an appointment, for any news at all, had no effect. Her stepmother replied that it wasn't a good time, that her father had to concentrate on his work, that they already had people staying or, when they set up home near San Francisco, that the change in climate wasn't good for the health, that the place they were living in the countryside was not much fun for children. One day, Eugene O'Neill wrote to her himself: "It has been too long since we saw each other." Oona was fourteen and hadn't seen her father for eight years. Invited to dinner at Tao House, her father's new property, Oona fainted at the table. The truth is that after his divorce he hardly saw her. The day Oona would meet someone as famous as her father, who would speak to her and accept that she listen to him, she would decide at once to sacrifice everything for him. Happiness is simple — take unhappiness and invert it.

But we're not there yet. For the moment, Oona is going to be sixteen. She is spending the summer with her brother and mother on a New Jersey beach called Point Pleasant, just south of New York. It's where her maternal grandfather bought an old two-story house on the corner of Herbertsville Road and Hall Avenue, surrounded by pine trees, at the point where the Manasquan River forks. It is there that her mother moved after the divorce. Oona grew up in this opulent melancholy. Her mother cried often while listening to Lena Horne. She dried her eyes with her back turned so that Oona wouldn't see her dry her eyes with her back turned. This is where Salinger will meet her again.

Oona spent the summer with her brother and mother on a New Jersey beach called Point Pleasant, where her maternal grandfather bought an old two-story house surrounded by pine trees, at the point where the Manasquan River forks. This is where Salinger will meet her again.

3
THE HEART OF A
BROKEN STORY

"Actresses are more than women and
actors are less than men."

Truman Capote

*I*f the moon was round and looked like a slice of
lemon, it meant life was a cocktail.

The waves of the Atlantic were breaking ceaselessly on the sand, a continuous breath, a liquid roar that
drowned out the footsteps of Jerry and Oona on the boardwalk as they headed toward Martell's Tiki Bar. Silences are
less awkward beside the sea.

What follows is an extract from one of Salinger's stories,
published in *Esquire* in September 1941 and never republished
since. It's called "The Heart of a Broken Story." I believe that
J.D. Salinger is writing what he felt the first time he saw Oona
O'Neill. It was the first time he found a voice similar to the
one he would use in *The Catcher in the Rye,* ten years later:

*"Shirley was reading a cosmetic advertisement in the wall panel
of the bus; and when Shirley read, Shirley relaxed slightly at the
jaw. And in that short moment, while Shirley's mouth was open,
lips were parted, Shirley was probably the most fatal one in all*

The waves of the Atlantic were breaking ceaselessly on the sand,
a continuous breath, a liquid roar that drowned out the footsteps of Jerry
and Oona on the boardwalk. Silences are less awkward beside the sea.

Manhattan. Horgenschlag saw in her a positive cure-all for a gigantic monster of loneliness which had been stalking around his heart since he had come to New York. Oh, the agony of it! The agony of standing over Shirley Lester and not being able to bend down and kiss Shirley's parted lips. The inexpressible agony of it!"

The repetition of *agony* was perhaps a childish homage to the word *horror* as it appeared at the end of Conrad's *Heart of Darkness.*

"The Heart of a Broken Story" imagined different versions of a meeting that never took place, the words that the love-struck man was incapable of pronouncing. *"In a boy-meets-girl story, the boy should always meet the girl."* In the end, Justin Horgenschlag stole Shirley's purse in the hopes of seeing her again. He was arrested and sent to prison, and from his cell he wrote her impassioned letters but was shot and killed by a guard during an escape. Jerry had this vision of love at twenty-one years old, when he dreamed of Oona at night: Love was more beautiful when it was impossible. Absolute love was never requited. But love at first sight existed. It happened every day, at every bus stop, between people who didn't dare speak to each other. The beings that loved each other the most were those who would never have the chance to love each other.

"Loving you is the important thing, Miss Lester. There are some people who think that love is sex and marriage and six o'clock kisses and children, and perhaps it is, Miss Lester. But do you know what I think? I think that love is a touch and yet not a touch."

Love was a touch and yet not a touch. That was one of the most perfect definitions of burgeoning love. It also chimed with one of Hemingway's novels: *To Have and Have Not.* It was in "The Heart of a Broken Story" that Salinger invented this kind of tender self-mockery—the character of the romantic and poignant young dropout who would seduce readers across the world in the 1950s. Before the war, Salinger already hung on to the idea of the individual abandoned in the big city, of the eternal adolescent who was passionate, selfish, and clear-headed, poor and free, transfixed with love, and utterly frustrated, who became the absolute cliché of the Western human condition in the twenty-first century. Salinger was extremely proud to have this story published by Arnold Gingrich in *Esquire.* Five years earlier, the same guy had published three of F. Scott Fitzgerald's autobiographical fragments, known as *The Crack-Up.* We currently live in the Salingerian epoch of proud indecision, of penniless luxury, of nostalgia for the present, of conformism to the indebted rebellion. We have an infinite hunger for pleasure, for happiness, for love, for recognition, for tenderness. And this hunger will never be sated by simple consumption, or consoled by religion. Justin Horgenschlag made a grand declaration of love to Shirley Lester, but before he did so, he swiped her purse! His letter was sent from prison. She didn't reply. (Or rather, in the story she replied politely, but at the end we learn that her letter is imaginary.)

The world is currently inhabited by horribly independent, neurotic, and unsatisfied beings. Lovers incapable of loving, sheep who refuse to be sheep, but who graze nonetheless, fantasizing that they are separate from the flock. Excellent clients for Freud, Buddha, Fashion TV, and Facebook.

Jerry Salinger couldn't foresee all this future waste, but he felt, if confusedly, that something was going to happen when, in the summer of 1941, he visited a friend of Oona's mother, Elizabeth Murray, whose brother he knew at school. He wanted to see Oona again—her angelic face, her high cheekbones, her mutinous dimples, her startled-doe eyes. Her "celebrity" side irritated him a little. Oona was finally chosen as the Stork Club Glamour Girl, and the picture she had taken with old tie-wearing men appeared on Page Six of *The New York Post*—what could be more vulgar than that? It was as if today she had accepted to take part in a reality show. The "Debutante of the Year" went on to pose for adverts in which she exploited her father's fame: *"The magic of a Woodbury Facial Cocktail...keeps Oona O'Neill's complexion fair and fresh."* The press conference at the Stork was one of Oona's biggest mistakes. In the middle of the war, she posed with an enormous bouquet of red roses in her hand. Sherman Billingsley, the boss of the Stork, slipped her a glass of milk so that he didn't have any problems with the cops. A tired journalist asked Oona what her father did for a living. Without getting flustered, she replied: "He writes."

Another journalist asked: "How did he react when you were picked as Debutante of the Year?"

Oona: "I don't know, and I'm not going to ask him."

Another journalist: "What do you think about what's

happening in the world?"

Oona: "With a world war raging, I think it would be out of place for me to sit in a nightclub and express my opinion."

Discovering Oona's photo in the *Post,* her father made a single public declaration: "God deliver me from my children!" Then he wrote a letter to his lawyer, who handled the alimony he paid to Agnes O'Neill: "Oona is not a genius. She's just a spoilt, lazy, frivolous brat who so far has proven nothing except perhaps that she is more idiotic and badly raised than most girls her age." He also wrote a very cruel letter to Oona: "All this publicity you've had is the wrong kind, unless your ambition is to be a second-rate movie actress of the floozie variety—the sort who have their pictures in the papers for a couple of years and then sink back into the obscurity of their naturally silly, talentless lives."

This less-than-flattering portrait would do little to prevent Jerry from suffering another respiratory episode when he saw Oona for a second time, on Point Pleasant Beach. He

Be a Beauty to your Soldier Boy
Here's how Deb does it!

"*The magic of a Woodbury Facial Cocktail...keeps Oona O'Neill's complexion fair and fresh.*"

knew that she had read Fitzgerald, and how could he resist the danger of a slender sixteen-year-old brunette who had read Fitzgerald? She was dressed in black again, but this time in pants and a knitted baby-doll dress, proving she was not the kind to take three hours choosing her evening wear. This girl made him asthmatic. They sat down in a bar overlooking the ocean with Elizabeth and Agnes, Oona's mother. Her childlike grace, her svelte figure, her milky complexion made him grit his teeth. He had noticed that every time something moved him, whether it was a human being or a kitten, he gritted his teeth really hard, like a sadist. At first this second meeting was a flop. Imagine that you're the New York it-girl and your mother is introducing you to a tall, scrawny guy who is having trouble breathing and won't stop gritting his teeth.

"We've already met. Don't you remember me?" No, she didn't remember their first meeting in the Stork Club. You should never ask socialites that question. Of course they don't, jackass! They met three hundred people every night. Jerry was mortified. While the two women ordered tea, he started talking about his lessons at Columbia University, the writing class with Whit Burnett, editor of *Story* magazine.

"So, what's the famous Whit like as a teacher?" Oona asked.

"He arrives late, reads one of Faulkner's stories aloud, then leaves before the end," Jerry answered.

One point to Jerry—Whit Burnett was a friend of Oona's father. She was angry with her father for never having taken care of her but couldn't rein in an unhealthy curiosity about everything he did. Jerry couldn't really admit that part of the reason he was attracted to Oona was because she was

Oona was chosen as the Stork Club Glamour Girl, and the picture appeared on Page Six of The New York Post. It was as if today she had accepted to take part in a reality show.

*Jerry started talking about his lessons at Columbia University,
the writing class with Whit Burnett, the editor of* Story *magazine,
who was also a friend of Oona's father.*

the daughter of one of America's greatest living writers. He was not proud, but why deny it? He was restless and impassioned. He was afraid of repeating the shy silence of last time so tried to impress her by describing Burnett, who published his short story "The Young Folks" in his magazine.

"He refused a whole bunch before. Then suddenly he gives me twenty-five dollars. That's the first time I made any money from writing!"

"If someone pays you for what you write, that either makes them crazy or you a writer," Oona said, with the patronizing tone of a schoolmarm congratulating a good pupil. "Above all if that someone is Whit Burnett."

In the months between the Stork Club and Point Pleasant Beach, Jerry had time to catch up: He read everything by Eugene O'Neill. He goofed by complimenting Oona on the gap between her *legs,* when he meant to say her *teeth,* and then Oona spilled her beer all over the Tiki Bar's table. He burst out laughing, mopping up the puddle with his shirtsleeve. For the first time, she came down to earth. They were two pouting extraterrestrials—she sulky, he intense. The mother and her friend had finished their iced tea and stood to go. They would finally have a quiet moment to drink alcohol alone, as Benny Goodman sizzled on the radio in the background. She looked at his hands with their long, fine fingers resting on the table. She wanted to touch one of them. His palm looked soft, and she told herself that she'd like to check if this was really so. At sixteen years old, touching a boy's hand wasn't binding. (At forty, it's a little more serious.) She was about to do it when he took on a disapproving look.

"Forgive me for coming back to this, but...what was that

Debutante of the Year thing all about? Didn't you know the Stork Club would use you in all their commercials like that?"

"No. Well...I mean...yes. It was some friends who organized it, so...I know, it's wacky! It's because of this farce that my dad thinks I'm using his name to have a good time and to get myself invited everywhere...which, strictly speaking, I am! He's never there. I should at least be able to use my name how I want, right? Anyway, he's never said a word to me in his life, so if he never speaks to me again it won't change a thing. Here, look at the letter he sent me."

From her bag she took an envelope covered in severe cursive, the kind of writing that wanted to demonstrate its importance through the shape of the consonants and vowels alone. The kind of envelope it was frightening to open because it was just bound to be notice of an IRS inspection or a subpoena. She read it aloud:

"I don't want to see the kind of daughter you've become during the last year. The only news I have of you comes from the tabloids." The corners of her lips drooped. She lifted her head and continued. "If you had a daughter, would you write her something like that?"

"I don't know. Maybe he wants to shock you, to stop you from becoming one of those society floozies. It's proof that he's not indifferent to how you lead your life, no matter what you might think."

"Nonsense! He's only thinking of himself. I'm dirtying the O'Neill name. He couldn't give a damn about me. He's just afraid of seeing his writer's prestige muddied in the society pages. You have no clue how little he cares about me. Your parents, I suppose, are still together?"

"If it'll make you happy I can ask them to get a divorce."

Oona shrugged. Jerry was wearing a gray coat with a black velour collar. It was called a Chesterfield, just like the cigarettes and couches. It was too tight, and his arms were longer than the sleeves. It was starting to look a little out of date. But Jerry was more self-assured than before: His first publication had given him the confidence he lacked. He saw himself as the hero in a novel. Would he take the plunge? You bet.

"Finish your beer, Oona, order a vodka martini, and talk to me about things that matter. I don't want to gossip. I'm trying to get to know you. What the hell got into him? Why did he ditch you? Just because you run out on the mother doesn't mean you desert the kid! I'm going to tell you what I think: I think your father is a great tragedian in everything, including his family life. He can no longer see the difference between his life and his art. You can see it in his latest play: He's speaking about himself. He's using his unhappiness—and yours!—as fodder for his work. What I'm getting at is that he's a towering writer, but a tiny, pathetic person."

Oona was stunned. Nobody normally spoke to her about her father except in the most glowing terms. She felt her eyes prick with tears, brought her hand to her mouth, got up, and ran out of the coffee shop—not to escape Jerry, but to hide her sobs. Jerry paid the check and followed her. He grabbed her arm. She turned around and...wow, she cried really well.

"I'm sorry," he said. "I didn't mean to bully you.... OK, maybe I did mean to bully you a bit."

"Forget it. You're right. I'm just fed up with how people always talk to me about him."

"You started it. Don't be mad at me for being interested in

Gene. I... I'm curious about you. There's nothing wrong with that, right? I like you. That's how it is. If you want, I'll make tracks right now and you'll never see me again. Just say the word and I'm gone."

"What word?"

"See ya!"

"That's two words....Stay."

She understood that she had to deal with another tearful suitor. Oona found them trying, the worst kind of pick-up artist, but the only nice ones too. The others were: the pale, suicidal rapist; the cruel Don Juan; the show-off who was always boasting about past conquests; the passive-aggressive who would insult you so you could knock him back, just as he feared; the antierotic joker; and, of course, the narcissist, the most painful kind, along with the repressed homosexual. But the tearful suitor was the most heavy going of all.

"How well she smiles after tears!" Jerry said to himself. He wanted to bite his tongue until it bled. He wanted to plunge his fingers into that innocent mouth. He wanted to peel this clueless little rich kid. Her voice was sweet, husky, hoarse,

melancholic. She was the kind of girl who spoke while looking out to sea. The gulls barked—I'm not kidding, they really did go "bow wow," like dogs strafing the beach. Let's listen in a little closer to what Oona said by the water's edge:

"Gene...my father, I mean...I hardly know him at all. I swear. I've seen him more often in photos than in real life. I haven't read his plays. When people talk to me about him, I act like I know what they're saying, but in fact, I've no idea who this guy, my father, is. I share the famous name of a stranger who poses in the newspapers and then scold myself for doing exactly the same thing. He scrammed to Bermuda when I was two to rehearse *Strange Interlude*. Tommyrot! He should have called it *Permanent Interlude*! I always felt like a burden to him. He could never bear his kids. He always just thought we were a hassle. If I bumped into him in the street today, I'm not sure he'd even recognize me.... Oh, shit!"

She looked at Jerry, then turned away, and her chin started trembling uncontrollably. She was mad at her inability to talk about her father without breaking down.

"Now you understand why I don't like to talk about him?" Oona said. "It's crazy. I should be able to control my emotions after all this time. Oh, shoot! He's really going to be a pain in the ass for the rest of my life!"

"I don't know if I prefer you when you're crying or smiling," Jerry said.

"Well, I hope you prefer making me smile," Oona said. "Otherwise we're not going to get along."

"Because you want us to get along?"

"Stop worrying, Jerry my boy. Of course we're going to sleep together tonight. We'll get it out of the way so you can

move on to someone else."

She smiled again, cruelly. She had the upper hand back. Jerry shut up. Damn, she was good! Immured in her sweet, high-society teenage solitude, proud of her sorrow and her milieu. The way she swung between tenderness and cynicism was irresistible. Did she do it on purpose? A girl opened up, then closed again: The problem was finding the right password. The more beautiful, famous, and spoiled they were, the more difficult their password was to crack. Seducing them demanded sophisticated espionage techniques that Jerry wouldn't learn until 1943, another two years yet, in the intelligence division of the 12th Infantry Regiment, 4th Infantry Division.

They walked along the beach toward the pier. The Atlantic Ocean was still grumbling in the background, which was useful for filling the gaps in their conversation. The gulls

laughed, seeming to mock the odd couple—a tall, dark man with a little elf. The wind lifted the sand, laying it to rest in their hair and eyelashes. If this were a movie, they would be filmed with a long tracking shot. This stylistic technique, oft used by Woody Allen, is known as the "walk and talk." Fortunately, then, Oona started talking again, because walking *without* talking is more like something from Bergman.

"Listen," she said. "I was lying earlier when I said that I didn't remember you. I know who you are. You're the mysterious giant from the Stork. We often talk about you, me and the rest of the Orphan Trio. Truman nicknamed you the Martini Moocher."

"Hey! I thought the owner was picking up the tab!"

"Of course! I'm just razzing you. Capote likes to say bad things about people he likes. That's how he shows his affection. I read your work in *Story*. 'The Young Folks.' It was like you took notes on our evening together."

"I did take notes on our evening together."

"Can I be frank with you?"

"Err...It's always a little scary when somebody asks that."

"Your writing is funny, but we can't say where you're going with it. Everyone's at cross purposes. The boy and the girl circle each other but never meet, is that it? What's the point in that? Apart from sneering at youth and explaining to everyone that rich kids are all idiots who think of nothing except drinking and fucking...."

"That's it! You understood perfectly!"

"Well, in that case, Fitzgerald got there first...and did it better."

"I'm just starting out."

Jerry couldn't hide his humiliation. He sighed as he ran his hand through his hair, fingers spread, a gesture supposed to mean *I'm above all that* but which Oona read as *Who does this little floozy think she is?* The Point Pleasant winds were drowning out the howls of the flying dogs.

"It's fine," she said. "You're just cutting your teeth, so don't pull that face. It's already great that you got published at your age. You know Truman turned green when he heard you'd been published before him. I thought he'd caught hepatitis! You want to know what he said? It's not getting published that counts, but getting published in *The New Yorker*[3] ."

"Capote looks like a fetus!"

"It's not nice to make fun of short people!"

"I'm not making fun. It's just an observation. He's an unfinished human being. Unless he's a troll, of course. As a

---

3. Truman Capote's first published story, "My Side of the Matter," appeared in *Story* in 1945, the same magazine that published "The Young Folks," J.D. Salinger's first text, five years earlier, in March 1940.

troll, he's swell."

"Stop being mean about my best friend, Mister Martini Moocher!"

They talked and walked, and walked and talked. Jerry bought two beers and a bag of popcorn from the kiosk. They threw popcorn to the gulls, who caught it in midair. Oona laughed heartily as she drank from the bottle, just like Jerry's part-Irish mother did, which was perhaps one of the unconscious reasons behind their attraction. The Irish had that little something extra. They were sexy, like the English, but more alive, less snobbish, more real, less haughty. They laughed harder and had bigger breasts and more freckles on their cheeks. They drank more too. A barrel organ started up beside them.

"Spare me!" Oona cried. "I hate mechanical music."

They put some distance between them and the machine—an ancestor of David Guetta—and approached a lantern-lit dance hall where a jazz group was swinging.

"It's too hot to dance," Oona said.

"Let your hair down."

"If I let it down, I become too pretty. I can't allow myself to do that this evening."

"Why not?"

"Because then everyone will want to sleep with me. It'll ruin our night."

Jerry didn't know how to dance, so they danced badly, but for a long while. The jazz sextet beneath the lanterns took turns playing solos, their instruments, silver and gold, sparkling beneath the painted lightbulbs. Oona stuck a flower in

Jerry didn't know how to dance, so they danced badly. The jazz sextet took turns playing solos, their instruments, silver and gold, sparkling beneath the painted lightbulbs. At that time, dancing was the only legal way of getting close to someone else. Dancing undid Oona's hair—her bun came apart, and her hair rained down over her shoulders.

her hair. Jerry's was slick with sweat. He took off his jacket, and their bodies wrapped around each other. At that time, dancing was the only legal way of getting close to someone else. The orchestra roared louder than the ocean. Dancing undid Oona's hair—her bun came apart, and her hair rained down over her shoulders. The flower fell to the floor, and they trampled it savagely, singing, *"I can't dance, got ants in my pants."* The song went on:

> *Let's have a party,*
> *Let's have some fun,*
> *I'll bring the hot dog*
> *You'll bring the bun.*

Exhausted, delighted that they had been able to transform their shyness into sweat, the couple returned to their now-tepid beers, which daubed handsome white mustaches on them both.

"You don't like to please, do you?" Jerry said.

"No. It's *that* that pleases me," Oona replied.

She laughed at her own jokes, not because she was self-satisfied but because she was afraid she wasn't funny. Jerry didn't ever know if Oona was joking or if she was being sincere.

"You dance almost as badly as I do, and God knows that's difficult," she said.

"I wanted to kiss you, so I danced badly on purpose so that we would come and sit down sooner."

Oona pretended not to have heard him, but a few seconds later they were out on the boardwalk, arms around each other's waists. Oona criticized his cologne and his haircut.

"All you think about is seducing thousands of girls," she said.

"Will you marry me?" Jerry asked.

"Not a chance! You're too young!"

"Look what I've got in my pocket. I think it belongs to you."

Jerry plunged his hand into his jacket and took out the Stork Club ashtray. Recognizing it, Oona laughed even harder and blushed for the first time that evening. Jerry furrowed his brow like a police officer:

"Miss O'Neill. I charge you with nocturnal ashtray theft."

"Hey! Technically I didn't steal it. You walked out of the Stork with this china in your pocket."

"Which makes me a fence! Thanks for the gift. Don't worry, if the coppers had arrested me I wouldn't have squealed on you. I would have gone to Sing Sing alone. Do you think they'd have let me take my typewriter?"

"If you give me a smoke we can flick the ash into it."

"Good idea."

A match crackled—two additional red lanterns in the twilight. Jerry noticed she wasn't inhaling the smoke. Their silences grew shorter and shorter. The air was warm, the night stretched out along the sand, the lamps on the boardwalk, like a daisy chain, took it in turns to illuminate them. They walked in front of the beachfront movie house, which was showing *Gone With the Wind*.

"Hey," Oona said. "What do you say?"

"Already seen it," Jerry said.

"They say it's better than the book."

"Huh! I don't see the point in shutting myself up in the

dark for three hours when I could be looking at you. You're prettier than Vivien Leigh. All you have to do is close your eyes and imagine that I'm Clark Gable and I've come to give you a ridiculous green bonnet."

"You know that Scott Fitzgerald worked on the script for that movie?"

"They can't have kept much. Poor old chap! You know his death really hit me hard."

"Everybody thought he was dead a long time ago, and maybe he was. Look, Jerry, I think I'm going to let you kiss me. But on one condition: It can't mean anything."

"Come on! Do I look like the kind of guy who thinks his actions mean anything?"

He leaned in toward her but didn't dare go all the way. She stood on tiptoe to close the gap. All of a sudden she felt lifted off her feet, both literally and metaphorically. They kissed, she floated, and he carried her. The dizziness was unexpected: This first kiss could have tasted of stale tobacco, but as Jerry breathed in Oona's perfumed hair (it forever had this sweet taste), she inhaled the fragrance of cinnamon soap from his neck. When two tongues touch, sometimes nothing happens. Other times, something does that makes you want to melt, to disintegrate, as if, eyes closed, you enter the other person, to mess everything up from the inside. He held her mouth tightly against his, holding his breath. After he landed her on the boardwalk, she only wanted one thing: to take off again.

"Everything seems to be in order."

"Perfectly. Perhaps we should start over?"

And how pleasant it was to start over! They started over a

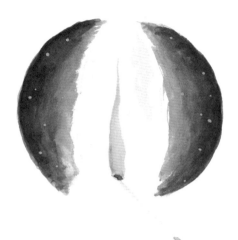

lot. Each time they kissed, she felt like she was flying, and he felt like he was falling down. It was a miracle they were still able to stand.

"OK, so instead of reliving the Civil War, how about we finish all the vodka back at your place listening to Cole Porter records? No funny business. We'll stay in your living room. Your mom will go to bed, and we'll dance to 'Moonlight Serenade.'"

"First, 'Moonlight Serenade' is not Cole Porter, it's Glenn Miller. Second, there's no vodka at my place, just white wine. Third, I was lying when I said I was going to sleep with you."

"I know. Lovely Dead Girl at Table Six."

"Excuse me?"

"It's the title of the story I'm working on right now. I'm hoping *The New Yorker* will take this one."

"You're crazy!"

When two tongues touch, sometimes nothing happens.
Other times, something does that makes you want to melt,
to disintegrate, as if, eyes closed, you enter the other person,
to mess everything up from the inside. He held her mouth
tightly against his, holding his breath. After he landed her on
the boardwalk, she only wanted one thing: to take off again.

"I know that too. Are you hungry?"

"Never."

"Why me?"

"Excuse me?"

"Why did you choose me? You've got all New York lining up."

"I didn't choose you. I let myself be chosen. There's a difference. Don't sulk! Kiss me again before I change my mind."

Let me remind you, and this is important, that on this evening Churchill begged Roosevelt to join the war, to help encircle Hitler, who had just invaded Russia.

In the living room of the old Point Pleasant house, Jerry and Oona invented a game: Obey the Song. For example, listening to "Night and Day" ("Only you beneath the moon and under the sun...") outside, beneath the moon. "Smoke Gets in Your Eyes," while exhaling cigarette smoke in each other's faces, "Cheek to Cheek"...well, you get the picture. Luckily, Oona didn't own "Stormy Weather."

Her mother, Agnes Boulton O'Neill, was very liberal. She trusted Oona and, anyway, had no authority over her. Like a lot of divorced mothers at a time when it wasn't done, she felt so guilty for the failure of her marriage that she forgave her daughter everything. Jerry couldn't believe he was there, in the dimly lit living room of the famous Oona O'Neill, completely alone, for hours on end, with the most beautiful teenager in New York, who was holding a glass in her white hand, who was looking at him, listening to him, answering him. He knew that it was a rare opportunity, one that perhaps he would never have again. (And in a way he was right; this evening would never happen again.)

"Why didn't you call me?" Oona asked.

Jerry couldn't tell her that he didn't have a phone in his student room.

"I wanted to write you a letter that would make you fall in love with me," Jerry said.

"Aren't you disgusted by people's bodies?"

Sometimes he felt like he understood her better and better, that she really liked him, and then suddenly—*wham!*—she'd close up, refuse to kiss him, without saying anything except "People's bodies disgust me" or "Anyway, you're just like all the others" or even "The only thing you find interesting about me is my father," to which he retorted that Eugene O'Neill's only real masterpiece was his daughter. These moments, when she put him to the test, were horrible. Suddenly, just as at the Stork Club, he wanted to get up and go home alone. He felt like a gangly loser. Not Mister Martini Moocher, but instead Mister Fed-up-being-dizzy-with-this-dame! And every time she felt she'd gone too far, Oona became sweet again, kind and affectionate, like the innocent orphan she was. The wind in Ireland must blow both hot and cold.

"I don't want life to be mapped out for me. Do you understand that, Jerry? The ordinary life… it's just not possible. I'd never cope. I want something else. If that's life, then… then it's not enough."

"What *do* you want?"

"I want to be the happiest girl in the world." Oona spoke this sentence as if she had said "You will be taken from this place to a place of execution, and you will be hanged by the neck until you are dead." There was no right of appeal.

Each time they kissed, she felt like she was flying,
and he felt like he was falling down.

night and day

Jerry and Oona invented a game: Obey the Song.
For example, listening to "Night and Day" ("Only you beneath the moon
and under the sun...") outside, beneath the moon.

"I'm going to start acting, you know?" she went on. "I was scouted by Cheryl Crawford, directrice of the Maplewood Theater. That's what the whole debutante, glamour girl thing is about. It's like when we kissed earlier and I let myself get carried away. It's ridiculous, I know, but it's better than continuing studying nonsense that will never help me get anywhere."

"You're not a starlet, deep down...."

"Oh, shut up, *poète maudit!* No, I'm afraid of this long existence that stretches out in front of us, and I don't know what to do with it. I feel like I'm on a cliff edge. Do you know exactly what you want to do with your life?"

She was leaning on the railing overlooking the rumbling ocean, as if she was watching her infinite future, as if the ocean was the hereafter thundering toward her, its cruel waves crashing in a foamy spray.

"I know I want to write the Best Novel Ever Written about Manhattan," Jerry said. "I don't want anything else. I want to mix Fitzgerald's emotion, Hemingway's concision, your father's violence, Sinclair Lewis's precision, Dorothy Parker's cynicism..."

"You really think you're something, don't you?"

"Writing isn't a profession for the humble."

"And yet you forgot to mention the best of all."

"Who's that?"

"Willa Cather."

"Yeah! I may be pretentious, but I'm not *that* pretentious! You can't beat Cather or the Brontë sisters."

"Will you write a role for me?"

"OK. How about an annoying little broad who doesn't

know what she wants from life? It doesn't surprise me that you want to work in the theater. You're always putting on a show."

"Is that so?"

"It is. You act naive, when in fact you're not."

"Twit! Just because I don't sulk all the time like you."

"Your sadness... it comes out anyway. It always finds a way out. That's what makes you charming. You smile all the time, but your eyes are crying out for help."

Oona changed the subject. This girl was a fighting machine. It really is an injustice that sixteen-year-old girls are always more mature than twenty-two-year-old boys.

"If you're going to write, you need to find somewhere quiet, outside of the city," Oona said. "My father writes in a cabin at the end of his garden."

"Oh, yeah?"

"Of course. He hates journalists and never goes out. Writers don't live in the world. They shut themselves away in little houses to write. Otherwise, they're not writers; they're clowns. The expression 'New York writer' is a contradiction in terms."

She was constantly sizing him up. The moment always comes when a man in love feels like a jobless bum at an interview. He was trying to score points with each sentence. When Oona smiled, it was like he was holding a winning lottery ticket. He had to stop himself crying "Yes!" She threw her cigarette into the garden. After a few seconds, it was difficult to pick it out among the glowworms in the grass. They transformed the lawn into a galaxy.

"It's normal that you're wondering about your future,"

Jerry said, "but I don't have that luxury. You're forgetting about the war. We're sending money and arms to Europe, but that won't be enough. Soon we're going to send men, and I'm going to get myself killed."

"Will you go over there, Soldier? To fight for freedom? I couldn't give a damn about freedom. It doesn't interest me. I believe in slavery!"

"Stop talking crap! Are you drunk?"

"An O'Neill is never drunk!" she said, raising the index finger of her right hand and a bottle in the left. "Hmm. All right. Maybe a little. Let's open another bottle... for the freeeeeeedom fighters!"

"I'm not going to spend the whole war holed up at my parents' place, that's for sure."

"My hero! I'll walk you to your ship, wave my lace hankie on the wharf."

This time she pressed her head against Jerry's chin. He tried to stand firm, even though he felt as brittle as this sixteen-year-old nymphet, with her awkward questions. Every time he laid his hand on her waist to dance, it was as if he was pushing a switch: Laying a hand on the black wool automatically made Oona open her mouth. And the harder her hip was pressed, the wider her mouth opened. A very practical system. Outside, the air smelled of hot dogs, of fries, of the iodine sea, of Saturday nights.

How cute the two of them are there. I love imagining them on the terrace of this old New Jersey house, the moon reflecting on the far-off ocean. I'm writing this on the other side of the same ocean, in Biarritz. We're face-to-face. I'm watching them, despite the seventy years that separate me from that summer evening in 1941, despite the Atlantic, despite their deaths. I see them turning around and kissing and arguing.... Kissing and arguing—that's the secret of happiness. "Love is a touch and yet not a touch."

Love is having and not having. When Werther chanced to touch Charlotte's foot, he didn't do it on purpose: It counts, and at the same time doesn't count. Love is born of an involuntary caress, of an uncontrolled slip. It's like speaking to someone on the telephone: The person is both there and not there.

Love is pretending not to care when, in fact, we care a lot. It's looking without finding. This little game, if played well, can last a lifetime.

They share a slow dance. It's very rare that two slow dancers want the same thing: Generally, one wants them to sleep together, while the other, head turned away, is politely waiting for the song to end....

(Something strange just happened. While imagining Jerry Salinger and Oona O'Neill at Point Pleasant, I decide to take a break, turn on the TV, and I see... Point Pleasant Beach, battered! Hurricane Sandy has just blown through. The planks of the boardwalk, where Jerry scooped up Oona in his arms, have been lifted up like blades of straw and piled like a game of pick-up sticks. The cottage swimming pools are full of sand. The Ferris wheel has toppled onto the beach, and the boats have been deposited on the roofs of houses, in gardens, beside blue slides and torn-up trees. Cars have smashed through living-room windows, carried by six feet of water. The streets are lakes. A grand piano sits in the middle of a roundabout. An overturned freight container blocks the road. The cars have turned into submarines. Utility poles have been snapped like matches. A strange turn of events: The moment I decide to tell the story of love striking Point Pleasant, a hurricane strikes the exact same spot. In October 2012, none of the scenery of summer 1941 remains. It's like what happened with *Windows on the World*. It's weird: Every time I write about America, the set disappears.)

A few hours, two bottles of white wine, and a packet of cigarettes later, Jerry's and Oona's heads were spinning. Falling in
love for the first time can have that effect. It feels so good, it
is exhausting, and then suddenly comes the fear of not being
up to it—that is the moment to leave. Lifting her index finger
solemnly, Oona started speaking again:

"Soldier Salinger. I've never been so afraid of anyone. You
look like a killer."

"You're right. I'm going to strangle you. That way I will
miss you...and mope. I like moping. It's my favorite hobby. I
practiced all my childhood. Nobody ever gave me a compliment when I was a kid except *he's got sturdy little legs.*"

"You do have sturdy little legs! Can we mope together?"

"Sure. Welcome to the Mopers' Club."

Beneath her marble skin, there were palpitating organs,
complex pipes full of blood, of bile and acid. Behind that face
were muscles, nerves, and bones. He wanted to peel her like
a pear, to see her veins, to disfigure this angel so that he was
no longer held prisoner by her face. To chew her like gum
made from human flesh. It's undeniable that, if he had never
become a writer, Jerry could have embarked on a brilliant
career as a serial killer. After all, he inspired a few.

"I like to mope too," Oona said, turning her glass about in
her hands. "When you leave for the war, I'll mope in a black
silk dress. I'll be extremely austere. I'll hang my head, and
everyone will come to console me. I'll look lost, out to sea,
and a doctor will prescribe me bicarbonate of soda. You little
bastard! I want to be your widow so much!"

Both extremely drunk, they discovered a shared darkness.
Nobody else at that time had such black humor: Kurt Cobain

and Marilyn Manson (both future readers of Jerry's) hadn't yet been born. Oona knew how to stay completely still while saying strange things. In the end, perhaps she was right to want to become an actress.

"I would give a shattering speech at your funeral," Oona said. "You would be posthumously decorated. People would compliment my devotion, shake my hand with pity. I can't wait to blubber on your tomb, Jerry. Then I'll marry a rich Brazilian, and in exchange for the material comforts he'll provide me with, he'll have my youth and the intellectual aura of a Nobel winner's daughter........." (The triple ellipsis comes nowhere close to capturing the uneasiness that followed.)

"You really are a filthy whore! How I would love to be relieved of your existence. Every night I dream of a wonderful world in which Oona O'Neill doesn't exist. Every second of my life has been hell since I met you."

"Thank you! Bring on the war!"

"Here's to the war!"

They clinked glasses without knowing that their macabre demands would soon be met, beyond all hopeless imagining. Then Oona set down her glass and started almost strangling him with both her hands, glaring at him without blinking, as if she were starving.

"That's it! I've drunk enough to talk frankly to you. Come on! Say it! I know you've been holding something back for months. Come on! I'll help you get it out. Repeat after me: *I... love...you...Oona.* Go on! I'm used to it, and it'll do you good. It's just four little words: I, love, you, Oona."

"I love you, Oona. My whole life is ruined. Loving you is suicide, Oona. I'm down. I'm out. Nobody has ever been so happy and so pathetic. I wish both my legs had been amputated so that I had never crossed your path."

"And voilà! That's good.... You're relieved, see? Now, listen to me. I accept your love. I will keep it preciously. Look me in the eyes. I don't know how to love, but I can let myself be loved by you, and only by you, and here's why: because you listen to me, captivated, when I'm talking nonsense."

"I can act too, you know! But it's a deal! One day I'll write the most beautiful novel of the twentieth century. Until then, let me take care of everything, little Oona. Loving you is easy. That's how it is. Nothing can be done about it. It should be compulsory."

She kissed him with her eyes closed, pressing up against him with exaggerated enthusiasm. I suppose that a professional novelist would describe the seascape and the wind, the clouds and the dew-kissed lawns. But I'm not going to, for two reasons. First, because Oona and Jerry couldn't give a damn about the scenery. And second, because they couldn't see a thing, morning not yet having broken.

"It's funny. When you kiss me, I feel as dizzy as when I'm riding the elevator to the top of the Empire State...."

"That's because you're drunk, honey."

"Oh, Lord! My head's spinning. I think I'm going to faint...."

Suddenly, Oona started retching, screamed "Oh, my God!" ran into the house, and flew up the stairs four at a time, with her hand over her mouth, before locking herself in the upstairs bathroom. The vodka-beer-wine mix has always been forbidden on a first date, but kids don't necessarily know that, even if they have Irish roots. Jerry heard the unromantic hiccups coming from behind the door. He went in and found himself alone on the first floor, in the dark living room. He stroked the French novels in the bookcase. Should he stay or should he leave? He didn't know how to help Oona without being discourteous. He heard her belch: "My father is the Empire State Building!" Her mother woke up, came out of her bedroom, and joined her in the bathroom. He heard them speaking.

"Oona?" Jerry shouted from the bottom of the stairs. "Do you want me to help you brush your teeth?"

After a long silence, during which the blackbirds started singing in the trees outside, Agnes, Oona's mother, came down to see him.

"Oona's not feeling very well. I think you should go. She wouldn't want you to see her in this state."

Jerry found himself behind the closed door without having the time to say anything except "I'm sorry. Tell her I said goodnight. My respects, ma'am..." Before closing the door, the former Mrs. O'Neill (who also stank of booze) added calmly:

"I gave her bicarbonate of soda. It works for everything. It whitens teeth, helps digestion. I even use it as a face mask. Oona is still a child, you know. She acts all worldly-wise, but in reality she's just a baby. You have to take great care of her. Do we understand each other?"

"Absolutely. But I..."

The door closed on his stammering.

As if it was his fault that she could only overcome her shyness by getting her dead drunk! He had thought an Irish girl could hold her liquor. Oona had made him forget she was only sixteen. Jerry noticed that it was daytime now. The nights are short on New Jersey beaches in the summer. The sun sets, then a few glasses later, it rises again. Here, someone like Sylvia Plath would add a light-riddled sentence like: "The simple morning sun shone through the green leaves of the plants in the little sunroom, making a clean look, and the patterned flowers on the chintz-covered couch were naive and pink in the early light." I like these pauses that give the reader a chance to breathe, to have a drink or a piss. Oh, if only I knew how to write like that! I'll just say that the first of the sun's rays was violet, and that it was pretty beautiful.

Walking alone on the Bradshaw Beach boardwalk, in front of the closed cinema, Jerry told himself that he would never again be as happy as he had been that night. A wholly perfect encounter... how often does that happen in one life? Once. Just once. You know that as well as I do.

Jerry scratched his head, repeating the same question aloud: "My God, what have I got myself into?" He breathed heavily and frowned at the same time. Kissing the girl you revere the most is certainly a victory, but what if that girl spews soon after? Perhaps it was the proof that he had stirred something in her. There were too many butterflies for her to digest! Or perhaps he had disgusted her, and from this day onward the name of Jerry Salinger would forever be synonymous with nausea. He didn't know if he should hope that she would remember everything or forget everything the following morning. Falling in love—just another dopey problem to deal with. Should he call or write her? How can he see her again without seeming clingy? How to be admired by the ultimate Manhattan babe? Jerry went to war long before his country did.

Delmonico's

4
THE TOAST OF CAFÉ SOCIETY

"It seemed like a nice neighborhood to have bad habits in."

Raymond Chandler (about L.A.)

Back in New York, Oona hadn't forgotten everything but acted as if she had no memory of the end of that night in Point Pleasant. Jerry would never speak of it again. They flirted throughout the autumn and winter of 1941 without ever mentioning her little gastric incident. It was the first time that either considered themselves "in a couple," yet they didn't hold hands in front of their friends.

In a famous old French movie, lovers say, "Paris is too small for such a big love." But here Manhattan was too big for their little love story. New York City can crush a love story with all its party lights, crazy musicians and rivers of alcohol. When you get older, you know love is precious, you learn to protect it. But they were too young to fight alone against the Big Apple's Forbidden Fruit.

First love is rarely the most successful, nor the most perfect,

The more Oona had fun, drank, blushed, played gin rummy with old codgers at the Stork, the more Jerry sulked in his corner.

but it remains the first. This fact is indisputable—neither of them would ever forget these beginnings. Jerry came to meet Oona outside Brearley School. They walked in Central Park, met up at Carol Marcus's enormous apartment on the corner of Park Avenue and 55th Street, or in coffee shops, at FAO Schwarz, or at the movies. They also had table six at the Stork Club, their bench in Washington Square, their favorite bookstore (Strand, Fourth Avenue), where they stole second-hand books and loudly recited the sentences that their former owners had underlined. Pressed close together, they fed the squirrels, kissed a little, and read movie magazines. You really have to be in love to read a magazine with someone—it is a little like the twenty-first-century couple watching television without giving a damn who has the remote. They bought cones of hot chestnuts on the way out of Bendel's department store, their pockets full of stolen trinkets. Between sixteen and twenty-two, we really know how to love. Love is absolute, free from the slightest doubt, the slightest hesitation. Oona and Jerry loved each other that way, without thinking, their eyes wide open. Sometimes he would slip his hand beneath her dress to stroke her young breasts through her bra, until she begged him to stop, and she would close her eyes to kiss him, holding him really tight against her as if she wanted him to continue.

"I never loved anyone before I met you," he said.

"Don't speak about what you don't know," she replied.

He read her his first short stories: "Go See Eddie," "The Heart of a Broken Story," "The Long Debut of Lois Taggett." She told him about the ingénue she had been cast as in *Pal Joey*. They spoke about their brothers and sisters, complained

Washington Square

about their parents (too present for him, too absent for her). They didn't make love when they slept together, just held each other tightly, in pajamas and nightdress, until they broke a sweat. Oona refused to take off her panties, and Jerry finished by coming into his briefs as he held back a moan. He respected her virginity. She would always tell him: "A child can't allow herself to get pregnant." He couldn't get over the fact she even let him hold her in his arms, slip the tip of his tongue into her red mouth, run his hands through her silky hair, scratch her bare back, fingers spread imitating spider legs climbing the spine, spending hours just feeling her trembling body against his, her breath on his neck and her marble arms. What a luxury! They may have been chaste, but Jerry and Oona were very sensual. It's difficult to understand in the twenty-first century, when we intertwine with each other just to say hello, but these vaguely intimate cuddles were enough for them. And there was no rush—she was too young to get married, and he acted blasé so she didn't feel smothered. When he caressed her, she sighed with her mouth half open, and he watched her sleep while counting the beauty spots on her back and pale shoulders. For him, gazing at her beauty spots was like watching the stars in the sky, giving himself up to a higher power. Jerry was a good-looking kid. He could have lost his virginity with any number of less timid girls. But he preferred to pamper this childlike starlet. The way she resisted his advances was a thousand times more erotic than a night with any old big-breasted tart called Samantha.

What information about sex existed in New York in 1940? Quite simply, nothing. No erotic pictures, porn photos, X-rated films, or sexual novels. There was no access to any kind of sexual user's manual, anywhere. It is the first difference you notice when comparing New York in 1940 with New York today, in which teenagers have unlimited and free access to all the pornography in the world. Despite being very attracted to each other, Jerry and Oona were scared stiff of making love because nobody had explained to them how to do it, or how to overcome their appalling lover's block. Jerry was too respectful to rush her, and Oona, for her part, was too intimidated to encourage him, and afraid of becoming pregnant.

As they couldn't see each other at Oona's place — she lived with her mother on Madison Avenue at the Hotel Weylin — they sometimes met in the room Jerry rented by the week, or more often at Carol's place. He had to be careful not to make any noise and would leave the apartment on tiptoe, closing the door gently, then walk home, a smile on his lips and frustration in his pants. The dissatisfaction only increased his joy, as it does for certain monks whose ecstatic faces are an excellent advert for chastity. Nothing prevented him from reaching lightning orgasm alone in his bed, thinking of Oona's insatiable kisses, the tautness of her skin, her baby scent, her milky complexion, her half-closed eyes, her little white panties, her little arched feet, her beauty spots, her pert breasts, her vampish teeth, her sighs in his ear, her fruity tongue, ooooh yesssss....

When she went out with her gang of friends, Oona sometimes came to join him in the middle of the night, to sleep by his side because she hated sleeping alone. She stank of liquor and cigarettes, but he was happy to welcome her to his rented poet's garret. She needed to talk, be pampered, covered in chaste kisses, reassured by his loving arms. She always said that she hated her body, found it small and plump, and despite his protests, asked him to turn out the light. Then she'd fall asleep in ridiculous positions, snoring or chewing on a corner of the pillowcase. Or she would play the princess, bossing him about: "Undress me, please. Brush my teeth, I'm too tired. Can you get me a glass of water?" Jerry didn't mind being treated like a butler as long as he could look at her slender feet. One night he drank champagne from her shoe. My God, how that pale foot arched as it slipped out of her pump, the varnished toes brushing against the leather and turning pink before being set free....

It's stupid, but at twenty-two you're proud that such a beauty chose you, even if it is just to fall asleep in your bed while you scratch her head so she purrs like a cat, while you get drunk on her fragrance of booze and smokes. When she

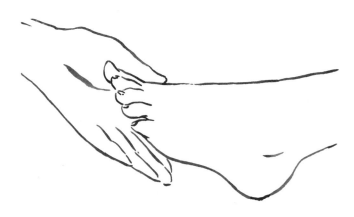

left, he would regret not having been more insistent with her. Did he have any idea that the kindness, the sweetness, and the back scratching were investments that would never pay off?

They also had the Stork Club dances. The party wasn't the same when you were dancing to jazz. In addition to the closeness of their bodies, the orchestra gave them something to talk about:

"Wait for the clarinet," Jerry said. "You'll see, the guy breathes poetry."

"No, the guitarist is much better," Oona replied. "His fingers can sing!"

"No way! Are you deaf? Listen to that drum solo! The boy is unbelievable! He strokes the skins with his washboard like he's touching a Negress' ass."

"Shut up for two-tenths of a second and enjoy the trumpet, you boob! This guy is spilling notes that can kill you in plain sight!"

Woody Allen was right: Everything changed with rock 'n' roll. We no longer expect every musician in the group to play his solo (except when that group is called Led Zeppelin). Before the invention of the discotheque, people really listened to the music, which was never the same twice. It wasn't just prerecorded background noise used to cover the void.

"Can you do the Charleston?" Oona cried.

"That old geezers' dance?"

"Come on, try it! You move your arm, and you throw both legs forward, but not at the same time. Otherwise you'll fall flat on your face!"

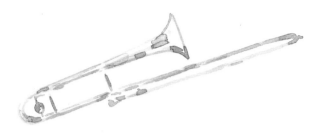

"She only had one fault—she was perfect. Apart from that, she was perfect," Truman Capote would write about his childhood friend Oona O'Neill in the 1970s, at a time when he was getting messed up in Studio 54, snorting coke by the spoonful as he watched young men smooch on the dance floor. It was the truth—the problem with Oona was her perfection. Because she hid her anxieties beneath excessive kindness, she was taking the risk that one day she'd crack (it happened to her at the age of fifty-two). Jerry wasn't perfect. He was bad-tempered and excessively ambitious. He was possessive, megalomaniacal, and irritable. These days of utter joy would only last a few weeks—the time for Oona to grow tired of this all-too-exclusive knight, and for him to realize (before her) that he was boring her and that their tastes, their hopes, and their lifestyles were strictly incompatible. He couldn't accept it, but he wasn't blind, and he knew deep down that Oona, having been ditched by her father, would never be able to love anyone, as she had had the courtesy to warn him on that New Jersey boardwalk.

"Why do you waste your time with these bozos?" Jerry asked one evening, when he could no longer hide his irritation. "Your girlfriends are stupid. They only think about getting drunk and marrying an old millionaire. Don't you see how empty their heads are?"

"Their company relaxes me," Oona said. "I like the fact that my Poor Little Rich Girls always pretend to be in high spirits. I need to take my mind off things."

"I need to take my mind off them!"

The lack of sleep was taking its toll on Oona. There was always a party at Carol's, with punch ladled out by domestics in white jackets who had earlier rolled up the living room carpet, while the parents were exiled to the upper floor. When she came to see him late at night, her eyes were wrinkled, her face was vacant, her teeth were painted gray by the red wine, and her hair stank of ash. That's what she'll look like if I marry her, Jerry told himself. I need to lose her so she'll remain innocent in my memory. Jerry's eyes wanted to be cynical but would never manage it. He was passionate despite himself.

"I can't go on watching you wither on the vine," Jerry said.

"If I'm going to stop seeing my friends," Oona said, "you'll have to cut off my telephone. Do you have any scissors?"

"You don't have to go running when they call for you."

"Can you imagine if everyone had a portable phone in their pocket? It would be a nightmare! We'd no longer be able to live. We'd be disturbed all the time."

"Stop changing the subject! You know full well that something so appalling will never exist. We'll always need a wire to connect people."

The posterior novelist is in a position to contradict his illustrious character on this point.

"Is a calm life possible with you?" Oona asked. "I mean, one in which we don't argue all the time?"

"I'm calmer than you are. It's you who wastes your time,

and mine, with that gang of hopeless night walkers."

"You're too serious. I love being tired, lying in all morning. Not thinking all the time. It's pleasant to sleep standing up. Problems slip away.... They are my friends; they love me; they're funny. We have a good time together. Is that such a problem?"

"You're not having a good time. Look at your face! They're taking advantage of your politeness to drag you into their alcoholism and superficial gossip. The truth is that you're incapable of being alone. You're scared to death of your own company. You flee yourself like the plague!"

"Are you done, party pooper? If you want to be a writer, you've got to relax a little. Have you any idea how much champagne Fitzgerald drank in one night? Enough to make him want to saw the barman in two just so he could see what was inside."

"And was the barman OK with that? Let me tell you something—*I'm* the barman, OK? And I refuse to let you cut my soul in two! See you around."

Jerry left, but he'd always come back. And Oona knew it. He could resist all manner of temptations but not the infinite suffering that Miss Oona O'Neill inflicted upon him. "Oh, the suffering! The suffering of standing close to Oona without being able to lean in to kiss her parted lips. The inexpressible suffering." This time, she caught his arm.

"You should follow my lead," she said. "Have a frivolous conversation and keep what's essential for your books. It's important for a writer to write, not to live."

"I refuse to waste my time," Jerry replied.

"You sound like my father, and he's the most depressing

man I've ever met."

"I know. He said it in an interview: Writing is my vacation from living."

When the three girlfriends had lunch at the Oak Room, the restaurant at the Plaza Hotel, amidst potted palm trees and the flashy gold decor, they really could be mistaken for the Andrews Sisters. In fact, Truman nicknamed them "Rum and Coca-Cola," with Jerry adding, "Working for the Yankee dollar"—effectively calling them hookers. Jerry was fed up with hanging out with this gang of alcoholic teenagers, but it was the only chance he had to see Oona.

She was sleeping more and more often at Carol Marcus's place, in the huge Park Avenue apartment, treated like a queen by the eighteen domestics, and barely leaving the sides of her two "adopted sisters," Carol and Gloria. People often asked them:

"Are you sisters? Triplets?"

"No, just lookalikes. But we don't know who's imitating whom."

"Individually we're awful, but together we're a calamity!"

Oona's mother let her stay out for the night from the age of fifteen, which gave her the time to write and to see her new lover away from her daughter's prying eyes. This tacit agreement worked for both of them, particularly since Shane (her eldest by five years) had run off to smoke joints in Bermuda.

"My mother sleeps around and gets depressed; my father lives in San Francisco and doesn't answer my postcards.... On the bright side, that makes me the freest girl in New York!"

The whole city swore by the trio of eminent young ladies—Oona, Gloria, and Carol—who dressed, made up, lunched, dined, danced, drank, and slept together. All three of them sparkled, with their painted eyes and parents' bank accounts. Jerry quickly understood that he'd be ill-advised to come between them. He had no other choice but to follow them around like a poodle.

Their favorite sport was to waltz up and down Fifth Avenue imitating Mae West's nasal accent.

Oona (pinching her nose): "I used to be Snow White, but I drifted."

Quoting this actress is not an innocent move: Oona admired her because she was the first femme fatale who treated male characters in such an offhand manner. Back in the day, it was customary for women to flutter their eyelashes lovingly. Mae West gave birth to the concept of the object-man, the boy-toy. Mae West revolutionized the feminine condition as much as Simone de Beauvoir did. Since Mae West, young guys daren't say "I love you" to young women, for fear of looking ridiculous or tacky.

Jerry didn't have the money for it, but because he was the oldest, he often picked up the tab, with increasing tetchiness, grumbling about the superficiality of this gang of good-for-nothings. As the weeks passed, Oona still refused to sleep with him and came up with phony excuses to see him less often. For example, she explained with an innocent gaze that she had spent the night dancing barefoot in the Vanderbilts' garden, listening to "Moonlight Serenade," and how much the song had made her think of him.... He could have choked her with anger! There was the rub—having followed her around like a lapdog, in her eyes he had become one. Of course, the more Oona escaped him, the more he wanted her. And the

*Oona admired Mae West because she was the first femme fatale
who treated male characters in such an offhand manner.*

Mae West revolutionized the feminine condition
as much as Simone de Beauvoir did.

more she had fun, drank, blushed, played gin rummy with old codgers at the Stork, collapsing in laughter and revealing her beautiful teeth, the more Jerry sulked in his corner, dark and taciturn, like a huge stork drenched in oil.

"You're crazy!" Oona said. "One moment you're happy, and then you flip your wig. In sixty years' time, they'll say you were bipolar, but for now you're just unpredictable. Like my father."

"It's you who depresses me," Jerry replied. "I don't know what to make of you. You can't call yourself 'shanty Irish' and then not give a damn about what's happening in Europe."

"Oh, here we go. He's harping on about the war again. Careful, we're going to get an earful."

"You want to have fun as if the crash never happened. But today all the flappers are either married or vagrants. Your father understood it, all right—the reason his plays are so dark is because all the partygoers committed suicide in 1930. Now is not the time for laughter. It's despondency and fear that sell now."

"Yes! I'm so sorry for being born in 1925. Let me just correct my date of birth."

"The party finished when you were four."

"And the war started when I was fourteen. What a gas! Thanks for the arithmetic lesson. But I'm not going to let Adolf Hitler ruin my youth."

Jerry chewed this over.

"I have to work on not being invisible. I want to be loved by this girl I hate. I want the scorn to change sides. In my writing, I have to be more monstrous than her. Love? Please, let's not be obscene. We're all gentlemen here. At the start

The Plaza Hotel

there was curiosity on both sides. Can this person hurt me? Love is the utopia of two solitary egoists who want to help each other make their sentence bearable. Love is a battle by the absurd against the absurd. Love is an atheistic religion. If it's temporary, so what? Life is too, after all. Oh, God, how I hate it when I see her, but how much worse it is when I don't...."

For a realistic understanding of what was passing through Jerry's head, try reading that last paragraph on a loop.

And then Oona looked at him and smiled, and he stopped thinking to gaze at the dimples in the contours of her cheeks. Sometimes she realized the power she had—he could no longer manage to hide from her that she had won the fight. He hoped for another war to free him from the one he lost every night.

In the end, Oona stopped kissing him back. He tried to slip his tongue into a closed mouth. The most painful thing was her politeness. Oona sometimes lay beside him all night, on the bed, fully dressed, immobile, silent and sad, and so as not to hurt him, she let him stroke her breasts without moving. A pretty girl, made as rigid as a statue by her lack of love, is perhaps the worst humiliation a man can face.

What happened during the winter of 1941:
—Fifteen brunches at the Oak Room of the Plaza to go over the horrors uttered by Truman the night before.
—Twenty-three drunken nights at the Stork Club, La Martinique, the Rainbow Room, Delmonico's, and the Copacabana.
—Four attempts to ice skate correctly in Central Park.

—Thirteen red-wine stains on the zebra-skin benches of El Morocco and twenty-two candle-wax stains on the white tablecloths of 21.

—A tour of French bistros (a sign of solidarity with the Resistance) at Café Pierre, Le Versailles, and Le Coq Rouge.

—Eighteen performances of the musical *Pal Joey* at the Maplewood, in which Oona made a brief but adorable barefoot apparition.

—Twelve afternoons shopping at Bloomingdale's, Bergdorf Goodman, and Macy's.

—Two balls at the Waldorf Astoria, another at the Roseland Ballroom, and a costume party at the Iridium Room at the St. Regis.

—December 7, 1941, 360 Japanese fighter planes destroyed 188 American planes and seven American ships on the island of Oahu, Hawaii, at Pearl Harbor, so called because of the pearl oysters produced there. The number of victims (2,335 dead) was almost the same as during the attack on the World Trade Center on September 11, 2001, sixty years later (2,606), which also led America to declare war.

What happened during the winter of 1941:
Four attempts to ice skate correctly in
Central Park...

...thirteen red-wine stains on the zebra-skin benches of El Morocco...

*...twelve afternoons shopping at Bloomingdale's, Bergdorf Goodman,
and Macy's...*

...December 7, 1941, 360 Japanese fighter planes destroyed 188 American planes and seven American ships on the island of Oahu, Hawaii, at Pearl Harbor.

5
WAITING FOR WAR

"It was this air of the spotless sky,
where shone so much glory, where
glistened so many swords, that the
youth of the time breathed. They well
knew that they were destined to the
slaughter.... And even if one must die,
what did it matter? Death itself was
so beautiful, so noble, so illustrious,
in its battle-scarred purple!"

Alfred de Musset

Confession of a Child of the Century, 1836

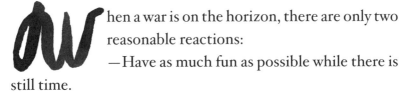hen a war is on the horizon, there are only two
reasonable reactions:
— Have as much fun as possible while there is
still time.

— Hole up in a shelter with supplies and weapons.

Jerome Salinger chose a third option. Called up to serve —
President Roosevelt having reinstated the draft — he could

have tried to escape his duty for health reasons. During his medical exam, the military doctor diagnosed him with a weak heart. Instead of taking advantage of this godsend to be declared unfit for service, Jerry insisted, going willingly to the recruitment office. The sergeant tried to dissuade him:

"You want to kill yourself some Nazis? You'll have to get in shape first."

He clung to the idea of the army as a way to avoid taking over his father's business. He didn't want to be a cheese importer and thought the war would give him something to write about—after all, Fitzgerald wrote his first book in the army.

4. All his life, F. Scott Fitzgerald complained of not having fought in World War I, like Hemingway or Dos Passos. After studying at Princeton, the future author of *The Great Gatsby* signed up for an officer's training camp, then became lieutenant in the 67th Infantry Regiment in Alabama, where he served as aide-de-camp for the general without ever

"Better a soldier than a cheesemonger," he told himself, how others of his age dreamed of being Coleridge or bust. His passage from Park Avenue to U.S. Army Intelligence wasn't a sign of his hopelessness but a way to achieve his dream of becoming Fitzgerald[4].

Jerry also wanted to show off his courage to raise his status in Oona's eyes. Having completed his studies in military

taking part in the fighting in Europe. Today, it's hard to believe that in the first half of the twentieth century, young Americans jostled to have the right to be shot at. (Note by the pen-pushing author who completed his military service in peacetime, for the French 120th regiment, winter 1987.)

academies, he was no brilliant Harvard graduate, but he knew the habits and customs of the American Army. He knew that the military life left a lot of time free for writing. Like everyone, he was afraid of the war, but not of soldiering. He also believed he'd be quickly promoted and so be less exposed than a simple private. He felt more at ease in military fatigues than in the suit-and-tie atmosphere of the Plaza, hanging out with celebrity orphans, and thought that in putting some distance between himself and Oona O'Neill, he could only become

more mysterious in her eyes. He fantasized about being the handsome boy in uniform, bidding farewell to his teary-eyed fiancée on the dockside, backed by the smoke of the ocean liner that would carry him to the south of England. Oona would have no choice but to crack at such a demonstration of virility and courage, like a princess in a medieval castle sending her valiant knight off to the crusades, after slipping the key to her chastity belt into his hand. Things didn't go quite as he planned. Oona didn't come to wave him off. On the last

night they would spend together, she announced that she was going to live in Los Angeles.

"You're going east, and I'm going west," she said. "That's what they call a modern couple. I'm joining Mom in California. It's better for my career. I'm going to take acting classes there. Please don't get burned up about it. I admire your sense of duty, but I have to get on with my life too."

What could he say? Oona's mother had left for Hollywood where she hoped to sell stories to the movie studios. Agnes Boulton O'Neill was working on a novel called *Tourist Strip,* and, because of housing restrictions imposed by the war, was living in a trailer. Gloria and Carol had also emigrated to the West Coast. Oona's departure was predictable...but Jerry, his vision clouded by the war, was blindsided.

"But...you'll wait for me?"

"Oh la la! Stop whining like that. You sound like Scarlett O'Hara."

"Don't you love me anymore?"

"I warned you I was emotionally handicapped. Stop asking so many questions. It's not the end of the world. We'll write to each other."

"It *is* the end of the world. Can't you see that? That's exactly what's happening—the end of the world! If this war doesn't look like the end of the world to you, I don't know what will!"

"It's too easy to say that. I won't follow you down that slippery slope."

"It's the truth! Everything is fucked up. It's horrendous. Our country just declared war on half the planet, and now you're breaking up with me, as if global tragedy wasn't quite enough. I don't give a damn. I'll die over there. That way you'll be rid of me."

"Hey! Don't switch things around. It's you who signed up. I didn't ask you to. How dare you leave me? Don't you want to see how this movie ends?"

"Please! Don't bring the movies into this, Miss Glamour Girl. Thanks for opening my eyes. You've always been an unremarkable actress. Your father was right. You have the same starry-eyed dreams as all phonies your age. You want to be famous? Bravo! Join ranks with all the other fireflies attracted by the neon lights of Sunset Boulevard. Come on, let's kiss one last time. I want to see you act the farewell scene. Lights! Roll camera! And...action!"

"Read my lips: GO. TO. HELL."

"That's exactly my plan for next year."

Their last kiss looked just like they do in the movies, when actors close their eyes and kiss with the corners of their mouths, pretending to love, waiting for someone to shout "Cut!"

April 27, 1942

Dear Oona,

I'm writing to you in a dapper and seductive uniform, begging your forgiveness. I was out of line the last time I saw you. I'm ashamed of my sentimentalism. I must have got this taste for melodrama from my mother, though I'm sure an Irish girl will excuse this ridiculous compulsion. I've just been billeted to Fort Dix, soldier number 32325200. Military service is a blast, on one condition— that you don't think too much. Sergeants hate privates who ask too many questions. A G.I. mustn't think. A soldier is a number who shoulders his rifle when the sergeant screams "Present arms!" The rest of the time—a mouth to feed, messy pack, dirty closet, chuck it all out on the floor and start again. Boot inspection, assembling and disassembling rifles, firing at targets, marching with a backpack that weighs a ton, learning to pitch a tent in a frozen hole. A good soldier falls asleep quickly at night because he just can't keep his eyes open. My problem is that I think about all the things we didn't

I've just been billeted to Fort Dix, soldier number 32325200.

get to do together, on Point Pleasant Beach or in my poetic bed. I remember the two of us in that old ladies' tearoom where I spent my month's wages buying you two cookies. I feel ashamed when I see us sitting under that tree in Central Park with your head on my knees, forcing you to listen to me read—pretentiously!—one of my unpublished stories. I'm holding the Stork Club ashtray against my belly. It's my lucky charm. I take it everywhere. A comrade is always asking me what I'm doing with a china ashtray in my pack instead of oranges and whiskey. I roll my eyes heavenward and answer: "It helps me mope." Usually he just shrugs and stubs out his cigarette on the Stork. I want to punch him, but then don't, because firstly, I'm a pacifist soldier, and secondly, he's built like a quarterback.

Whenever I have the time, I write my thoughts on this white letter paper. Forgive my rambling. It follows the threadless thread of my thoughts. Put this gibberish down from time to time and go to the living room to make yourself a vodka martini. I don't want to be a pain in the ass, but you should know that distance has turned you into a kind of demigoddess who occupies my mind like a Chinese brain teaser. I get so bored when I'm not thinking of your shanty Irish smile. It's long and tedious learning how to kill Germans, and yet, believe me, I'm in no hurry to get going with it! But idleness is eating away at us. There's nothing to do except rake over old happy memories, tell each other flippant anecdotes, conjure up images that make you smile sadly at night while the other guys fiddle with themselves under sticky sheets. The guys speak about their girlfriends, but I keep my mouth shut. I don't know if I have one or not. Do I have a lover? Oh, God! I'm off again. Heavy, heavy, HEAVY! You sent me a lipstick kiss on a white page, but I spilled coffee on it. I kept it anyway. It's as if your mouth drank that revolting dishwater. I'm sorry for being so SOPPY, but I like to think that we shared that disgusting beverage. How is the play going? The one not written by your father. I'm sure he'd hate Pal Joey. The story is too simple. Darling Joey, torn between the wealthy widow and the poor chorus girl. Of course, he'll choose the pauper, even though he'd be better off keeping both of them. You obviously want to drive your father nuts. He treats you like a bastard child, but you're not. In fact, deep down, you have the same stubborn, disobedient, free, and intolerable character as he. I'm sure he knows it. What exasperates him about you is himself.

What became of the Park Avenue Trio? Are Misses Marcus and Vanderbilt still as seductive in Hollywood? The colonel just passed by. He's the one who stands straight, hands clasped behind his back, *to make himself seem important. The sergeant is there for the screaming, but the colonel sows his fear silently. We call this system "The Army." It has existed for so long that nobody would dream of changing it. A guy marches quickly to impress the guy below him, who screams all the time to impress the guy one notch down, who shits his pants and picks up his stuff, emptied from his bag into the mud by the guy above, and cries at night because he's far from home and doesn't know when he'll see that farm again in Kentucky or Alabama.... Shit! It's so strange when you think about it, Oona. We have to march in time. I don't know if you can imagine me marching, but it's comedy of the first order. "Left, left, left right left," and we sing stupid military songs, and we have blisters on our feet.... And do you know what's going through my mind? "When they begin the Beguine." Believe me, I know how that must look on the page. SOPPY again. "When they begin the Beguine, it brings back the sound of music so tender," and I march to it, thinking of the St. Patrick's Day party, that crazy Irish night together at the Stork, spinning under floods of Jameson's. Oh, if only the American Army had the idea of ordering training songs from Cole Porter.... Little Oona, you save my life several times a day, and you haven't got the SLIGHTEST IDEA.*

Your U.S. Army hero kisses your cheek, your right eye, your left ear, then works his way down to your neck, with love and squalor.

Jerry

P.S. I sent my typewriter to the laundry.

Military service is a blast, on one condition—that you don't think too much. Sergeants hate privates who ask too many questions.

May 8, 1942

Dear Oona,

I was transferred to Fort Monmouth, still in New Jersey, for a six-week radio course. Don't ask me what it's about. I haven't the foggiest. I suppose the soldiers firing up front need to transmit information to those loafing about at the back. I've been taught how to scream into a radio microphone, install a telephone line, send coded messages. Perhaps my next letter will be written in an indecipherable language. Not that it will change much about my arcane style and the lack of a reply from you. Why the silence? I know that I write too much to you, but it's not because I'm idle. I think about your little face so much. I hope that you're not fright- ened of the war—thanks to me, neither the Germans nor the Japs will attack Los Angeles. I won't let them hurt you. Tell the Trio that I'm prepared to die for the Mocambo! I've been put in charge of the new recruits here, giving me several dozen slaves not to take advantage of. I always have your face in my sights. Can you bear Los Angeles? New York will never recover from its loss. I have the feeling that soon it won't just be me who sees your face in the dark- ness. Are you going to any casting calls for the movies? Isn't that too humiliating for someone who was born a star? I'm sorry for our arguments, my rotten temper, my obsession with the war, when we should have been happy. We went quite well together, right? Or did I ruin it all? My memory embellishes our past. It's a mental illness that ruins good times so they can be regretted later. I've got into the

dumb habit of idealizing you ever since I put on this virile uniform and was surrounded by these boy drinkers with their freckles and acne. I like them a lot and hope I won't change my tune. I
met a skinny kid who was crying in the hallway because he was
being bullied by a gang of assholes. Another defended him and got
beaten to a pulp in his place. You know, great things like that happen every day, and it gives you confidence despite it all. I asked
to be made officer, as a former cadet. We'll see, but I realize that
I'm only telling you this to brag. I'm still writing my little stories.
It's also for you that I write. My short stories are letters to Oona,
though twisted and disguised, which will maybe reach you if you
buy Esquire or the latest Story. There are my private letters and
these open letters, and they are all for you, to take or leave. I beg
you to excuse this excessive writing. I've been invasive ever since
I met you. I am your Adolf, and you are my France. Don't worry,
I won't ask for anything in exchange for my occupation of your
spiritual territory. Just be happy that you inspire me. It's not your
fault. It just fell upon you, and I know that we weren't made for
each other and our story was half-assed from the very start. I used
you as a Muse, and at the moment it's thanks to your absent presence, your puckish silence, that this writing is—stupidly, obsti-
nately—gaining ground within me. I'm going off to fight—if you'll
excuse my grandiloquence—not for the country or for liberty or the
good or any of that crap, but for your cheekbones, your blushes, your
big incisors, your soft shoulders, as silky as a peach. That will be
my war—me writing letters that you'll never answer. I don't want
you to answer. There's too much risk you'll tell me you don't like me

anymore. I'll write you all my life, and later, when my books are published, everyone will think they're novels because it'll be written on the cover. But you will know they are letters addressed to you alone.

Don't forget your heroic hero. His future invalid's pension will guarantee you a swanky life.

Jerry

I've got into the dumb habit of idealizing you ever since I put on this virile uniform and was surrounded by these boy drinkers with their freckles and acne. I like them a lot and hope I won't change my tunc.

6
THE LONG DEBUT OF OONA O'NEILL

"I hate movies like poison."

J.D. Salinger

rom the army, Jerry continued sending short stories to literary magazines. "The Long Debut of Lois Taggett" was published in *Story* in September 1942. Like "The Young Folks," it is a satire on the gilded youth of New York, their arrogance and empty-headedness. This time, however, we might speak about a short story *à clef*—"Lois Taggett" seems directly inspired by Oona O'Neill and her friends Carol and Gloria. Salinger launches a literary Pearl Harbor on them, similar to the bombardment to which Capote would subject them in *Answered Prayers*. Once again, Salinger was one step ahead of his rival:

"Lois wore a white dress, and orchid corsage, and a rather lovely, awkward smile. The elderly gentlemen guests said, 'She's a Taggett, all right'; the elderly ladies said, 'She's a very sweet child'; the young ladies said, 'Hey. Look at Lois. Not bad. What'd she do to her hair?'; and the young gentlemen said, 'Where's the liquor?'

"That winter Lois did her best to swish around Manhattan with the most photogenic of the young men who drank scotch-and-sodas

*in the God-and-Walter Winchell[5] section of the Stork Club. She
didn't do badly. She had a good figure, dressed expensively and in
good taste, and was considered Intelligent. That was the first season
when Intelligent was the thing to be."*

We feel a rising anger in Jerry against these spoiled Park
Avenue girls who continued thinking only of their pretty
clothes while Europe and Asia were put to fire and the
sword: *"It was the first big year for debutantes to Do Something.
Sally Walker was singing nightly at Alberti's Club; Phyll Mercer
was designing clothes or something; Allie Tumbleston was getting
that screen test."* As Salinger was yomping through mud, climbing ropes, and crawling under barbed wire, he had difficulty
stomaching the idea that his ex was still going out every night
to Los Angeles nightclubs with her New York gossip girls,
although I don't think that's the only reason for his severity
with Oona. He guessed that she was slipping away from him.
He was trying to make himself disgusted with her in advance,
as if to get a head start, before the inevitable breakup. "Little
Oona's hopelessly in love with little Oona," he confided to a
friend. Oversensitive men often behave this way. Better to
destroy the object of affection than to submit to its yoke. It
could be seen as a way to test the strength of feeling, although
above all it's a very effective way to fuck things up.

In "The Long Debut of Lois Taggett," Lois marries a handsome man who stubs out his cigarette on her hand and breaks
her foot with a golf club. Then Lois Taggett buys a dog whom
she abandons in the street a few weeks later because he took
a piss in her elevator.

Salinger, in love with Oona, wrote what it took to destroy

---

5. Walter Winchell was a famous columnist who specialized in gossip and tittle-tattle,
a kind of Perez Hilton of the 1940s. Oona was regularly quoted in his *New York Daily Mirror*
column, in which she was nicknamed "the toast of café society."

her before he was destroyed himself. Loving someone is much too dangerous. Jerry preferred to go off to war before he was tempted to make Oona suffer, or to suffer because of her. He was quite sure Oona wouldn't wait for him, which didn't mean he wasn't crushed when she replaced him with someone else.

Don't underestimate the role social neurosis played for this son of a Jewish cheese importer, besotted with the daughter of one of his country's most famous writers. He would, of course, have refused to admit he felt inferior, like Justin Horgenschlag in "The Heart of a Broken Story" or Bill with Lois in "The Long Debut of Lois Taggett." I love the definition of wealth Salinger gives at the end of this paragraph: *"Lois ordered a scotch-and-soda, drank it, and four more like it. When she left the Stork Club she was feeling pretty drunk. She walked and she walked and she walked. Finally she sat down on a bench in front of the zebras' cage at the zoo. She sat there till she was sober and her knees had stopped shaking. Then she went home. Home was a place with parents, news commentators on the radio, and starched maids who were always coming around to your left to deposit a small chilled glass of tomato juice in front of you."*

In the long run, the class war always trumps noble sentiments. Jealousy, insecurity, scorn—all the ingredients were there for a sublime, one-sided, passionate love. This impossible, lopsided story would grow during the war. It's the story of a love that only magnifies with absence—the young writer will fall deeper and deeper in love the more the war separates him from a fiancée he (wrongly) believes to be lightweight and superficial.

There is something of Gatsby and Daisy in this idyll between a social climber on a quest to purify himself and this white goose of "café society." Which of the two is the more innocent? Who suffers more? Because he's preparing for war, Soldier Salinger believes he can instill virtue in the Glamour Girl from the posh neighborhood. He's lying to himself, refusing to admit that he's just like Truman Capote, fascinated by this world of sequins, wealth, and fame. At the age of twenty-three, Salinger is an American Bel Ami, a New York Barry Lyndon. But he's wrong about Oona. She hangs around with poor little rich girls, but she isn't one herself. Her mother lives in a Los Angeles trailer park, and her father burned the bridges between them long ago. The only thing that Oona needed was to be consoled, taken care of, sheltered, not lectured about her superficial social life. This child, alone in New York, was looking for someone to protect her, to adopt her, like a cat who pretends to be independent, then demands its bowl of milk on a regular schedule. She couldn't be happy with a belligerent teenager, with an infantryman posted overseas, with a gloomy writer, and even less so with a shell-shocked veteran.... But to understand all of that, he'd need at least another twenty years.

After Jerry left for the barracks, Oona O'Neill took a train to join her mother in Hollywood. Carol, her best friend, had gotten engaged to the writer William Saroyan (she was seventeen, he thirty-three), and in 1941, Gloria had gotten married at the age of seventeen to the attaché-de-presse Pat DiCicco, thirty-two, a big drinker and gambler, and Howard Hughes's PR man. Oona was the last singleton of the Trio, her two best friends having chosen to marry men much older and more famous than themselves. They all moved to the West Coast at the same time. Their arrival caused a sensation in Los Angeles. Gloria Vanderbilt's wedding was one of the society events of the year; the other would be Carol Marcus's nuptials in Sacramento. As soon as she stepped off the train— which soldiers leaving for the war had drenched in beer— little Oona O'Neill was invited for dinner at Earl Carroll's by Orson Welles, who wanted (supposedly) to talk with her about his upcoming movie *The Magnificent Ambersons.* He was twice her size. Welles had just left Dolores del Rio after the commercial flop of his first film, *Citizen Kane.* Oona loved his deep voice but hated his nose. It didn't last long. It's impossible to fall in love with someone without liking their nose because it's always there, in the middle of the face, and gets bigger and uglier as time passes. Orson Welles would get over this disappointment by marrying Rita Hayworth the following year, before cheating on her with Gloria Vanderbilt. Beverly Hills is pretty small.

Something very strange happened the evening Oona met Orson Welles. At the end of dinner, Welles asked Oona if he could read her palm. Oona held out her hand, and Welles looked at it attentively, then declared that her love line indicated she would meet a much older man.

"That's original," Oona said.

"But I know who it is," Welles said.

"You, I suppose?"

"Not at all. I said someone you were going to meet, not someone you're dining with now. It's Charlie Chaplin. You'll meet him soon enough. And you'll marry him too."

Oona burst out laughing and paid little attention to this

drunken nonsense.[6] The fact that Welles cited Chaplin is not surprising; the two of them were very close. In 1941, Orson Welles offered Chaplin the main part in a film he wanted to direct about Landru, the French wife-killer. Chaplin liked the idea so much that he bought it from him and made *Monsieur Verdoux* in 1947.

Ben Hecht defined a starlet thus: "In Hollywood, a starlet is the name for any woman under thirty who is not actively employed in a brothel." If Oona never became a starlet, it is thanks to her father. At Gloria Vanderbilt's wedding, Oona found a good agent, Minna Wallis, the woman who had launched Clark Gable's career ten years earlier. A pretty girl with a famous name met all of Los Angeles' celebrities quickly—it was much less difficult than today. With her father's fame and her photo forever in the papers, Oona O'Neill had a greater chance of climbing the movie industry ladder than if she had been a waitress in a Sunset Boulevard bar. She read Jerry's letters but didn't reply to them. She knew that it was over between them and that he was becoming obsessed with this love story simply because he was holed up in a military dormitory.

And now we're going to try a furiously modern experiment. Together, dear reader, we are going to invent the YouTube novel. I'll tell you how to proceed: Find your computer, or an iPad, or any other dopey digital screen. Go to YouTube.com and search for Oona O'Neill. The search engine will offer you a black-and-white still of Oona wearing a headscarf. This one:

You can bring Oona to life by clicking *play*. In it, Oona is seventeen and freshly arrived in Hollywood. It is 1942. The treasure you are about to see is the first and last of Oona

---

6. This anecdote is confirmed by the English theater critic Kenneth Tynan and was told by Orson Welles during his televised interview with David Frost.

O'Neill's screen tests. It is for a casting filmed by Eugene Frenke for *The Girl from Leningrad,* a project in which Greta Garbo had already agreed to star. Oona was supposed to play Tamara, a young Russian, which explains the headscarf that

makes her look like a princess disguised as a Caucasian peasant. Watch the video and we'll talk afterward. And I hope that after a cyber-chapter like this, literature will never again be accused of having an allergy to technological progress.

So, you've discovered Oona O'Neill at seventeen. Admit that she literally devours the screen. The camera is in love with her childlike traits, while the director stammers. He addresses her as if he's speaking to an orphan discovered on the banks of the Volga. He asks her to turn her head so he can see both profiles, which are exquisite. She laughs— embarrassed, shy, impish, and irresistible. She has a fragility that sucks you in, despite the absurd headscarf that's hiding her dark brown femme fatale's mane. Watch her eyebrows placed like two apostrophes above her sparkling gaze. Listen to her crystalline voice when she asks, with queenly politeness, "Shall I turn over here?" Suddenly the team that is bossing her around seems like a gang of vulgar louts. They are all aware of what an honor it is to breathe the same studio air as this radiant and reserved angel. When she looks into the lens, for the briefest moment, thousands of different emotions are committed instantly to film. Oona knows that the situation is unpleasant. She's afraid of messing up. She thinks she's pathetic, would like to be somewhere else, feels embarrassed and clumsy, and yet is having fun at the same time. Her discomfort transforms into mischievousness, a feline charm, pure and sparkling—after all, it's annoying, but it's not really serious. In a fraction of a second, she transmits a score of contradictory emotions into the camera's eye: vulnerability, elegance, fear, modesty, politeness, lassitude, shyness, sweetness, kindness, confidence, desperation, solitude, etc. etc. Her face moves a lot. Perhaps she's too nervous and she can't guess what expression these cretins expect from her. She seems to be constantly apologizing for being there, while lazily accepting the compliments. When she appears to protest, crying "I don't know what to say..." with all the courtesy of a well-raised girl caught by her governess, we understand how all the men who met her at that time suffered: We want to, have to, take care of her. Otherwise, life is pointless. And when she looks to the heavens at the end of this miraculous video, she is amazing, divine—there is no other word. She's looking up to the very sky she fell from, which is also where she resides today. Faced with this apparition, what else was there to do but succumb? In these rarely seen images, Oona O'Neill crushes Audrey Hepburn as the frightened deer, Natalie Portman as the graceful faun, Isabelle Adjani as the emotive ingénue, Paulette Goddard in dazzling sadness, Louise Brooks as the fallen angel, Greta Garbo in languorous insolence, and Marlene Dietrich in poisonous chilliness... because she is natural and simple. Her sophistication is involuntary, without work or effort. On the contrary, she seems to be always fighting against attracting attention, which is the best way to win it. She could have had a beautiful career, become a star, a global and immortal icon. Oona is not a woman; she's a principle. Her beauty is ultramodern. Truman Capote was wrong. She's not perfect; she's better than that. So what happened? Here we plunge into the mystery of Oona, into what makes her great. A few weeks after these extraordinary screen tests, she definitively renounced all her cinematic ambitions.

As Oona's audition with Eugene Frenke had still not brought a response, Minna Wallis organized a dinner party to present her to the world's greatest cinema genius, who was looking for a young actress to play Bridget, the main character in a movie called *Shadow and Substance*. Charlie Chaplin arrived early at Minna's. Oona was sitting alone on the floor, watching the fire in the hearth. She was wearing a low-cut black top, which contrasted with the longer, more sober skirt, belonging to her mother. Oona's magic—violet lips, black hair, her father's sparkling eyes, her mother's straight nose—worked as usual. This is what Chaplin wrote in his autobiography:

"I had never met Eugene O'Neill, but from the solemnity of his plays, I had rather a sepia impression of what the daughter would be like.... While waiting for Miss Wallace, I introduced myself, saying I presumed she was Miss O'Neill. She smiled. Contrary to my preconceived impression, I became aware of a luminous beauty, with a sequestered charm and a gentleness that was most appealing." He knew at once that she would play an important role in his life.

Charlie Chaplin

Having only ever seen him in black and white, Oona was surprised by Chaplin's blue eyes. He was thin, attentive, short like her (five-foot-five), with that famous face (sans mustache), gray hair, and a strange way of moving, as if he was dancing. He was wearing a three-piece dark-gray suit and a blue tie, which brought out his eyes. He was fifty-four years old. He looked like the Tramp but elevated to the bourgeoisie—were there any other actors who became millionaires while playing vagrants? I don't think it would be possible today. Like all professional comics, Chaplin was very serious, almost sinister, but he tried to break the ice.

"Have you been in Los Angeles for long?"

"A few weeks. A friend of mine just got married, and my mother lives here."

"Minna told me you trod the boards a little in New York."

"Oh, nothing much, just a little role in a musical. I played the ingénue in *Pal Joey* last summer at the Maplewood."

"It's a good play. Why do you want to be an actress?"

Oona thought about this and blushed, because she knew it was an important question. Charlie sensed her discomfort. They were as shy as each other. And yet Charlie was a ladies' man (in truth, he spent much of his life with real pains in the ass who were only after his money and used him to break into movies). It was possible that Oona's shyness was catching: Every time she met someone new, there was silence. She got used to this phenomenon a long time ago and supposed it was her fault: In company, she was the expert at creating an awkward vibe.

"You don't have to answer," Chaplin said. "Perhaps my question was indiscreet?"

"Oh no, it's not the question that's the problem, it's the answer. I want to be an actress because I'm not interesting, because I don't know who I am, because I feel vague, hollow, empty, because if I'm asked to be myself, I don't know what that means, because I always want someone else to whisper to me what I have to say. I also want to be an actress so I can be applauded and loved by everyone, but that's a side issue really. There you go! Did I answer your question well, Mister Tramp?"

The young woman had turned scarlet, but her damp and piercing eyes were issuing a challenge. As Oona's and Charlie's eyes met, they welled up simultaneously. It would be unfit to talk of a *coup de foudre*...a flood would be more appropriate. If I were Boris Vian, I would write here what he said when Colin met Chloé in *Froth on the Daydream*: "An abundant silence spread around them, and most of the rest of the world faded away to nothing." Fortunately, Minna Wallis came into the room at that moment, otherwise the double drowning would have become really awkward.

"Sorry I'm late," Minna said. "Though I confess I took my time on purpose so you could get to know each other. What are you drinking?"

"A gin and tonic, please," Charlie said.

"The same, thank you," said Oona. "As an alcoholic's daughter, I can say that I have no problem holding my gin."

"Oona," Charlie said. "Can I ask you one more indiscreet question, after which I promise to leave you alone?"

"Yes."

"How old are you?"

"Seventeen."

"My goodness!" Charlie said. "I'm three times your age! Normally I could be the father of my actresses, but this is the first time I could be their grandfather!"

"I don't see what the problem is. I'm much more mature than you are."

"It's true! You don't walk around with holes in your shoes, a cane, baggy trousers, and a bowler hat."

"Neither do you, outside of office hours."

Charlie laughed, and he didn't laugh often at other people's jokes. Such complicity with one of the biggest stars of the time was only possible if the girl was completely drunk or dreadfully indifferent. Or an extraterrestrial. Charlie was spellbound: He had been living it up in Hollywood for thirty years but had never met an extraterrestrial, except perhaps Paulette Goddard, his last wife, with whom he had stayed the longest, and who was the most intelligent of the lot. Anybody who has read *Hollywood Babylon* knows that Chaplin liked young women and that this attraction had caused him many problems—trials, scandals, and gossip. One day, Chaplin boasted about having slept with more than two thousand women before he turned fifty. He had married his second wife, Lillita MacMurray, who, at the age of twelve, played an angel in his film *The Kid*. He had gotten her pregnant when she was fifteen, and on the day of their secret wedding in Mexico, she was sixteen and he thirty-five. After how the American press had gone for him at the time, he stayed on his guard when rattled by a younger woman. However, Oona's calmness reassured him. This girl wasn't trying to sell herself like merchandise, or to please him by fluttering her eyelashes like Betty Boop. She was well raised and discreet, and that was what he

Chaplin and his second wife, Lillita MacMurray, who, at the age of twelve, played an angel in his film The Kid.

needed after a thirty-year streak of bad marital luck—a little bit of candor. Not another vamp to take him for a ride, but a generous ingénue who didn't consider him an enemy: neither a playboy to tame, nor a bank account to drain, nor a director to convince, nor a future father of her children...at least not on the first evening.

"Now can I ask you an indiscreet question?" Oona said.

"Of course. Unless you're a journalist."

The joke tugged at Oona's dimples, particularly lovely in summer.

"I'd like to know if Hitler has seen *The Great Dictator*."

"Oh, I've got no idea! All I know is that he banned the film, in Germany as well as France. Naturally, I hope with all my heart that he has seen it. He stole my mustache, after all."

Chaplin said this as if it were the most natural thing in the world. As if announcing that two plus two equals four.

"Is that so?" Oona said.

"He started growing that little square tuft on his lip in the twenties, whereas I've had mine since 1914. He copies everyone. He stole the word *Führer* from Mussolini, who calls himself *Il Duce*. Yes, I think he did steal my mustache! It's all the more amusing because for me the toothbrush mustache symbolizes my character's vanity, just like the hat and cane."

"Except his is real!"

"True. Mine was always a postiche. How did you know that?"

"You said so in the *Los Angeles Sunday Times*. Why did you never grow a real mustache? Are you allergic to facial hair?"

Charlie smiled at her brazenness. This little pest certainly was a change from the brown-nosers at the Polo Lounge. The more they spoke, the more he felt that their age difference diminished.

"I want to be able to take off my mustache when the camera stops rolling. I take off my undersize bowler hat and my oversize pants, the size fourteen shoes, the bamboo cane… and the Hitler mustache!"

"But you didn't answer my question. Do you think Hitler has seen *The Great Dictator*?"

Chaplin burst out laughing at the young girl's insistence.

"I told you so, Charlie," Minna shrieked. "This little one's got character!"

"How to be certain? I think that Goebbels could have organized a private projection for him in Berlin. Hitler is crazy about cinema: All his public appearances are meticulously

"It would have been wonderful to be a little German fly on the wall when Hitler watched your Hynkel, juggling with the globe," said Oona.

planned, set up, and directed like movie scenes. Apparently he calls himself Europe's greatest actor, but I disagree. He over-eggs it. Visually, he is more influenced by his compatriots, Lang and Murnau. A mix of *Metropolis* and *Sunrise*! Did you notice the alternation between massive wide-angle shots and extreme close-ups in *Triumph of the Will*? It gives the impression of power, a drunkenness, a fever. I watched all of his propaganda films before shooting *The Great Dictator.* He may have borrowed my mustache, but I stole his megalomaniacal low-angle shots and all his body language—the raised chin, the nervy arm movements, the military flights. I had a lot of fun with him, even if I don't find him funny."

"Admit that it would be amusing to you if he'd seen your film," said Oona. "It would have been wonderful to be a little German fly on the wall when Hitler watched your Hynkel, juggling with the globe."

"I imagine that after a few minutes he would have left the room screaming—Jew! Degenerate art! Although I'm neither Jewish nor a degenerate."

"If there was a screening, everyone who organized it was probably hanged straight after," Minna said.

"It's true that he's not well-known for his ability to laugh at himself," Oona said.

"That's why I think he hasn't seen it. Anyway, I doubt the film would touch him at all. To write *The Great Dictator,* I read his *Mein Kampf.* He doubts nothing. He's not someone who thinks about himself; he doesn't have the time. He declares war on everybody else instead. The way he clenches his fists betrays his lack of self-confidence. I'm sure Goering reassures him. That's why I put a fatty beside him in the picture: Hitler and Goering, to me, are like Laurel and Hardy."

"Is it true you were born on the same day?"

"No. I'm four days older!"

"Four days? That's odd. He's like your double in a way. Your evil twin. I'm sure you know that he has blue eyes like you?"

"And we're more or less the same height!" Chaplin strode up and down the living room as if he were Adolf, imitating him in German-sounding gobbledygook.

"Und ich meßünzet dass ich gëfunt mein Kartoffeln!"

Oona and Minna almost snorted up their gin. Oona had

admired Chaplin since *City Lights,* that's to say, all her life. Like all children born in the 1920s, she grew up watching his films, in movie theaters or private projections at friends' homes. Her favorite was *The Gold Rush,* but she also loved *The Kid* and *Modern Times* for their social punch and their violence, similar to her father's work. Deep down, Chaplin's work was comic Eugene O'Neill. He always chose dramatic subjects — famine in the Klondike, orphans, poverty, the condition of the working man, totalitarianism. And in every film, he managed to transform the worst tragedies into something ridiculous. She was beginning to understand where she was and what was happening — something incredible that had never happened to her before, conversing with the man whose "lyrical feet" Scott Fitzgerald admired. The friend of Somerset Maugham, Eisenstein, and George Bernard Shaw. Remember that Chaplin dolls had been on sale for twenty years and that he ran United Artists, one of the largest movie studios, which he founded in 1919 with Douglas Fairbanks, Mary Pickford, and D.W. Griffith. Meeting Chaplin in 1942 would be like meeting someone today who was as popular as Rihanna and as powerful in Hollywood as Steven Spielberg. And despite the *Chaplinmania* that had followed him all over the world for the past three decades, Charlie's blue eyes were still alight, alive, attentive, and tender. Nothing was calculated. He was simple and spontaneous. Is it possible that an artist of such stature should be so easy to be around? Or was this the regular turn of a falsely humble old pickup artist? Without realizing it, Minna Wallis answered Oona's questions:

"Charlie, it's the first time I've seen you like this. You're literally glowing."

"I know what you want me to tell you: Is it thanks to you or thanks to Oona? Well, I refuse to fall into such a crude trap by saying that it's thanks to Oona."

Chaplin gazed at her. Oona lit up the room more than any lamp. She was tiny like him, and he could see she didn't have the body of a bimbo (or rather a "cover girl" or "pinup" as they said back then), but Charlie, like all movie directors, was only interested in faces. You didn't see the body on screen, at least not in 1942. The face, however, that was what caught the light.

After the dinner at Minna Wallis's, Oona went to Chaplin Studios uninvited to see him again. At first she was given the boot like any other groupie. Charlie was afraid of a new scandal. So Minna hassled Chaplin until he agreed to offer her a contract for a future film. Chaplin summoned Oona to his house on Summit Drive for cinema lessons. Oona got on very well with Charlie's sons (Charles Jr. and Sydney), who were roughly the same age as her. But she only had eyes for their father.

When news broke of Charlie Chaplin's new affair with the underage daughter of Eugene O'Neill, it caused a national scandal. The Hollywood gossip pages raked over Chaplin's troubled private life. Joan Barry had just started paternity proceedings against him. When *The Great Dictator* was released at the end of 1940, the American government was not pleased, because it was treading water, hoping to remain neutral in the war. Many American citizens looked favorably on Hitler, the horrors of 1917 having made them isolationists, or simply noninterventionists, owing to their pacifism. Americans had no desire to go back to war. When

*Eugene O'Neill's wife, the failed actress Carlotta Monterey,
hated Chaplin, who had never given her a role.*

Operation Barbarossa was launched, the majority thought
it best to let the Nazis and Communists kill each other off.
This turned a lot of people against Chaplin. And the wors-
ening climate of hostility only hastened his engagement to
Oona O'Neill—the fact that it was forbidden stoked his passion. For her part, it was her father's extremely violent reac-
tion that hurried things along. They were in the exact same

position as Romeo Montague and Juliet Capulet. As soon as they announced their engagement, Eugene O'Neill cut all remaining ties with his daughter and died ten years later, having never seen her again. His wife, the failed actress Carlotta Monterey, hated Chaplin, who had never given her a role. But above all, O'Neill couldn't bear the idea that his daughter had chosen a father to replace him. Charlie Chaplin and Oona O'Neill were two fatherless beings, for Charlie had never known his either. Later, Oona's two brothers would commit suicide. Eugene O'Neill Jr.—unemployed alcoholic, three times divorced—sliced open his veins in a bathtub in 1950. Shane, a junkie, threw himself from a third-story window of a New York building in 1977. Oona, however, came good, because Charlie made her laugh. Oona had to fight for her happiness. Nothing in her life was set up for that, and yet she managed it, that day. The forsaken child had found a protector, like Holly Golightly with her old Brazilian millionaire. Between the possible (Charlie) and the impossible (Jerry), she didn't hesitate for a second.

On the letter paper of the restaurant Musso & Frank, 6667 Hollywood Boulevard, Hollywood, California:

Dear Jerry,

I'm going to try not to be too complicated for once. You know that I have difficulty saying what's weighing on my stomach. Perhaps it will be clearer when I write, but I know that, upon first reading, this letter will seem cruel to you, and I infinitely regret that. Read my letter as many times as you need to. I have thought so much about each word that I now know it by heart.

Forgive me for not being worthy of your feelings.

I'm living with my mother in Los Angeles now.

In fact, I'm starting my life. I will be born in fifteen minutes.

I know that you're hung up on me because you are far away and because you are frightened. I'm frightened too, that we might not understand each other.

Something has ended between us.

You know I admire you. Your originality capsizes me, and I don't regret a single moment I spent with you, even the hours you kept me awake reading your work aloud!

You also know, I hope, surely, that it's finished between us. It's so obvious. If you don't see it, it's because you're being willfully blind or you're playing the role of someone far less intelligent than yourself.

I hate having to remind an American Army hero of that by letter. As war is coming, I should probably lie to you. But I can't do that anymore. Not to you and not now. You know it would be horrible of me. I can no longer live letting you think there is the slimmest hope, while you're off preparing to overthrow Hitler.

It's over between us, Jerry. It's a mediocre way to put it, but it's true.

You will always be a part of my past, but you are no longer part of my future.

"We possessed together the precious, the incommunicable past." You know that Mrs. Willa Cather is always right, don't you? I've finally understood what she means—that what we have lived through will never disappear. It's always there, and I will never forget it. When we met, when we danced, what we sang, and what we read. Our memories won't vanish. Maybe one day, someone will write a sentimental book about us!

What a terrible thing this clarification is.

I don't want you to suffer from a separation caused by Pearl Harbor.

But neither do I want you to write to me as if I'm your fiancée or future wife.

I'm sorry. I'm ugly and stupid and maybe...in love with someone else. Do away with me! Forget the little Central Park bitch, the dirty debutante. I'm not worthy of your courage. This is the first act of bravery in my short, anti-Semitic, Irish life! (I'm kidding!)

I'm standing to attention as I tell you, "At ease, soldier, you can grow!"

Take care of yourself. Don't die. Don't take pointless risks. You have to live if you're going to become a great American writer like my father.

Forgive and forget,

Oona

P.S. The Mocambo (L.A.) is much less fun than the Stork Club. Just as rotten, except the parrots are real. I promise, you're missing nothing.

July 1942

Dear Oona,

I read some good news and some bad news about you in the papers.

The good news was that you are finally paying attention to what's happening outside of the Plaza. You were very photogenic in that Life *magazine picture at the Lafayette Hotel, rolling bandages for the war in Russia. I also saw you in that shampoo ad, taking a foamy bath in your swimsuit by the pool, perched on that boy's shoulders. It's a pretty way to show your patriotism. Anyway, those pictures brightened up my gray barracks. To summarize for you what I've learned these last few months: In the war, we throw grenades instead of confetti. So you see, my life isn't so different from yours. What matters is throwing things into the air while making sure you're not standing under them when they fall back to earth.*

The bad news is the rumor of your affair with Charlie Chaplin. You're screwing an old Englishman with prostate problems who takes cantharidin to bring his worn-out old tool back to life. I don't know whether to scream with laughter of collapse in floods of tears at the shame of it all.

I should have strangled you the night we met. I almost did, but I was lazy. I did want to die in this war, but now I don't want to, because what would be the point? You wouldn't even miss me. Do you remember our drunken conversation on that hellish Point Pleasant boardwalk? You told me you'd make a beautiful widow, but how can you be my widow if you marry someone else? If I die, you'll be nothing and you'll remember nothing. Be careful, this isn't a marriage proposal, but a brief instant of revolt against your indifference. You quote Willa, but you forget what's important—"the precious, the incommunicable past" disappears forever when the person dies, and memories die with people. Every death is a great big pile of things rubbed out.

I'm now teaching student officers at the Air Force's aviation school in Bainbridge, Georgia. Weirdly, I like explaining to kids how to kill Nazis. The contact with the recruits has made me generous and kind. I'll end up as a high school teacher, with essays to correct, a corncob pipe, and a pince-nez. It's nice being responsible for others. I could grow to like it. I try to reassure them by promising them laudanum. I think I'm unable to leave the school. I like the atmosphere. I feel less lonely, and at the same time can drop everyone to go off walking in the countryside. I was right to be wary of you, but I should have been wary of myself too.

I'll leave you now because these dopes are setting fire to their farts with a lighter, and one of them has severely burned his asshole. As you can see, this war is damned dangerous.

I'll take official leave of you now, my messed-up shanty Beverly Hills Irish girl. You were my laudanum. Quitting you is like an amputation.

Jerry

Distant Oona, I thought of you as I boarded the Queen Mary *for England. You swore you'd come and wave a white hankie on the dockside, do you remember?*

January 18, 1943

Distant Oona,

I thought of you as I boarded the Queen Mary *for England. You swore you'd come and wave a white hankie on the dockside, do you remember? My mother tried to fill in for you, but she cried too much. The shame of it! I hope your pregnancy is going well. We crossed the Atlantic with the 4th Infantry Division. We'll be training in the south of England. Damn it! I can't hold back. You have to know that your husband is a deserter. Chaplin escaped two wars because he's a coward. We're going off to fight, something he's never done. Don't you care that you married a man without any balls? A man who dresses up as a bum because he was never made to wear a soldier's uniform?*

I've kept the Stork ashtray. I fill it up with ash and wads of used chewing gum. The best present you ever gave me was stolen from a nightclub—that should have set me thinking. You never gave me anything that was truly yours. You had nothing to give. You were empty.

Love never destroys anyone. It's stupid to believe something like that. Our nonstory is already rubbed out. I have understood and digested that catastrophe. You never massacred me; you only made me old. But don't expect me to forget you. You taught me everything. It's because of your cruelty that I understand women. I grew up at top speed, like a flower photographed every day that wilts in twenty seconds in a flipbook. I was afraid of you once, but if you knew what I think of you now, it's you who would be afraid. I want to thank you for saving me time. I grew up ten years for every week I spent with you. Thanks to you, I'm turning 230 tonight, and the kids in my dormitory who are fighting over a dodgy round of poker have no idea that they're sleeping beside their great-great-grandfather. I'm writing this hunched over my pillow, huddled up like an old man on my flea-ridden mattress. Thanks, Oona. Thanks for your coldness. It toughened me up. Perhaps the war will finish off the education you began. I wish you a long and happy life with your deserting movie star.

Signed he whom you once called "Ooh Jerry, Jerry" when he was nonchalant and luminous. Apologies for no longer being enchanted. You jaded me. Soon I'm going to look like Franklin Delano Roosevelt in his wheelchair.

Careful not to travel on a cruise liner, I heard that German submarines are torpedoing them right up to Manhattan.

This letter is not signed.

Summit Drive, Beverly Hills, June 1943

Dear Jerry,

Your last letter disgusted me. You are being so unfair, and I just don't know how to respond. I was fifteen when I met you. I was (and still am, as are you) much too young and stupid to know anything about love. We messed around together for a while, and it was charming, but life pulled us apart, just like every day it pulls apart millions of lovers just as sincere as we were. You want me to feel pathetic, repugnant, and to believe I'll burn in hell because, like all New York flirtations, ours had to break up one day or another. The only reason I decided to reply to you was because of your current situation. I beg you, on my knees, to be careful, to not play the hero, and to come back in one piece. Even if you feel like disobeying me, and even if we never see each other again, it's better for you that you don't come back crippled if you really want to write your Manhattan Masterpiece. Focus on that instead of your poor little tart, married to a crumbling celebrity. I prefer to ignore what you say about Charlie and to put your unfair slurs down to your disappointment. Write and survive— that's all I ask of you. I will be so proud to read your books after this appalling war. Note down everything you see in the notebooks I gave you. This is my last letter, but I hope from the bottom of my heart that it does you good, because I never wanted anything else. I refuse to be angry with you. I wouldn't manage it; my nasty remarks would just ring false. I regret to inform you that I am incapable of thinking bad of you in any way whatsoever. So stop insisting! You will never diminish the pride I have that I knew you and that you will always be—vaguely, absurdly, tenderly—among my memories. You are my only chance of entering the history books except as the wife of a movie star! Please don't show this letter to anyone. The gutter press would have a field day. I know that you won't because you have, even in that violent and insomniac dormitory, remained the elegant young man I knew in Greenwich Village who made fun of the way I gossiped with Truman, Gloria, and Carol, and who always wanted to take me to see films where everyone killed themselves at the end. Do you remember? I never liked those easy epilogues. They insulted our imagination. There is always a better solution.

Your little madam who sends you a kiss despite everything, as soon as her husband's back is turned (toward the flashbulbs!).

Oona O'Neill Chaplin

7
TOO YOUNG
FOR YOU

"The salute with the hand
thrown back over the shoulder,
the palm upward, made me want to put
a tray of dirty dishes on it."

Charlie Chaplin

This is what J.D. Salinger wrote in a letter made public during a trial brought against his first biographer, Ian Hamilton: "I can see them at home in the evenings. Chaplin squatting gray and nude, atop his chiffonier, swinging his thyroid around his bamboo cane, like a dead rat. Oona in an aquamarine gown, applauding madly from the bathroom. Agnes in a Jantzen bathing suit, passing between them with cocktails. I'm facetious, but I'm sorry. Sorry for anyone with a profile as young and lovely as Oona's." (Salinger v. Random House, U.S. Court of Appeals 2nd Circuit, No. 86-7957; January 29, 1987.)

He is reproaching Chaplin for doing just what he would do his whole life. It would be the last time that Jerry fell in love with a woman his own age.

I don't understand why some people find it shocking for a

mature man to be attracted to fresh young flesh, when that's how Plato describes the ideal couple in his *Symposium*.

For fun, I made a list of famous couples with a large age difference:

—Hugh Hefner and Crystal Harris (sixty years' difference)

—Johann Wolfgang von Goethe and Ulrike von Levetzow (fifty-five years' difference)

—J.D. Salinger and Colleen O'Neill, a nurse and Oona's homonym, whom he married in 1988 (fifty years' difference)

—Georges Clemenceau and Marguerite Baldensperger

(forty-two years' difference)

—Liberace and his driver Scott Thorson (forty years' difference)

—Pablo Picasso and Françoise Gilot (forty years' difference)

—Jorge Luis Borges and Maria Kodama (thirty-eight years' difference)

—Muhammad and his third wife, Aisha (between thirty and forty years' difference, depending on the historian—the first time he met her, she was playing with a doll)

—Rubens and Hélène Fourment (thirty-seven years' difference; when they married in 1630, she was sixteen, he fifty-three)

—Charlie Chaplin and Oona O'Neill (thirty-six years' difference)

—Woody Allen and Soon-Yi Previn (thirty-four years' difference)

—John Casablancas and Aline Wermelinger (thirty-four years' difference)

—Bill Murray and Scarlett Johansson in *Lost in Translation* (thirty-four years' difference)

—Roman Polanski and Emmanuelle Seigner (thirty-three years' difference)

—Johnny Hallyday and Laeticia Boudou (thirty-two years' difference)

—Witold Gombrowicz and Rita (thirty-one years' difference)

—Colette and Bertrand de Jouvenel (thirty years' difference)

—Frank Sinatra and Mia Farrow (thirty years' difference)

—Nicholas Ray and Natalie Wood (twenty-seven years' difference)

—Paul Nizon and Odile (twenty-six years' difference)

—Humphrey Bogart and Lauren Bacall (twenty-five years' difference)
—Humbert Humbert and Dolores "Lolita" Haze (twenty-five years' difference)
—Romain Gary and Jean Seberg (twenty-four years' difference)
—Adolf Hitler and Eva Braun (twenty-three years' difference)
—Bret Easton Ellis and Todd Schultz (twenty-three years' difference)
—Alfred Stieglitz and Georgia O'Keeffe (twenty-three years' difference)
—Johnny Depp and Amber Heard (twenty-three years' difference)
—Pierre Abélard and Héloise (twenty-two years' difference)
—Peter Bogdanovich and Dorothy Stratten (twenty-one years' difference)
—Guy Schoeller and Françoise Sagan (twenty years' difference)
—Serge Gainsbourg and Jane Birkin (eighteen years' difference)

When I asked Paul Nizon why we are attracted to people younger than ourselves, he thought for a moment before replying:

"There are two reasons," he said. "Skin and renewal."

The American press went to town on Chaplin, labeling him Bluebeard. His first film after the war, *Monsieur Verdoux* (1947), was almost called *Barbe bleue*. It was a terrible flop, both with the critics and the public.

Today, all actors over fifty years old have "underage" wives.

Oona O'Neill Chaplin spoke elusively about this subject in an interview with the *Daily Herald,* Provo, Utah: "Charlie has made me mature, and I keep him young."

I should remember to ask those "Girls who marry older men"—besides material comfort, is it really the calmness and serenity that reassures them? Or is it the fact that they have already achieved their professional goals on this earth, already slept with all the women, already quenched their thirst? Is the mature man a Buddhist sage, faithful, sated, and reassuring?

Bullshit. It's much simpler than that. The mature man chooses a young woman because she is guaranteed, until his death, to make him short of breath every time he sees her leave the bathroom. And the young woman is happy to be so admired, particularly if she has daddy issues. In the twenty-first century, the innumerable cohort of fatherless girls provides an ample breeding ground where disgusting old leches can have their fill. No further explanation is needed to know why they are mysteriously attracted to mature men: For certain young women, love consists quite simply in finding a man capable of replacing Daddy. Young boys don't admire young girls enough. Twenty-year-old men have too many things to do than worry about taking care of a woman. Oona fell in love with Charlie because his ambition was behind him. Chaplin fell in love with Oona because her life was in front of her. Indeed, from the moment they met, he was so happy, he could only make terrible films. He never really succeeded in the transition to the talkies: In *A King in New York, Limelight,* and *Monsieur Verdoux,* he overacts, soliloquizes, gives great teary speeches, willfully exaggerating his English accent to irritate American ears. When Chaplin made his debut in 1910, cinema was a funny distraction, a little like a magic trick or a circus turn. Thirty years later, he had mastered the most powerful art form of all time. He had gone from being a clown to being a star—something that really went to his head in the twenties and thirties, even if he had recently come back down to earth. Getting old has a calming effect on everyone, in particular the pretentious, because the approach of death makes them modest—they have found something stronger than them.

In *Graziella,* Lamartine summarizes everything in a formula: "Ah! The young man is incapable of love. He knows the value of nothing. He cannot appreciate true happiness until after he has lost it. There is more wild sap, more fluttering shade in the young plants of the forest; there is more fire in the old heart of the oak. True love is the ripe fruit of the lifetime. At eighteen years, one does not know it; one only imagines it. As in the vegetable nature, when the fruit comes, the leaves fall, so perhaps it is in human nature."

Oona fell in love with Charlie because his ambition was behind him.
Chaplin fell in love with Oona because her life was in front of her.

8
THE LONGEST YEAR
JUNE 1944–APRIL 1945

"Yea, thou shalt be as he that lieth down in the midst of the sea."

Proverbs 23:34

Utah Beach, Normandy, June 6, 1944, 6:44 a.m. Nobody in his regiment slept the night of the fifth and sixth of June. It was on this beach that Jerry landed seventy years ago, from one of four thousand boats, flown over by eleven thousand planes. Fortunately, unlike Omaha Beach, Utah didn't give onto a sheer cliff. It is said that Operation Overlord stank of vomit—everyone was seasick in the landing craft, and those who weren't threw up with fear. Jerry's battledress was splattered with hunks of bacon and coffee, barely digested by his neighbor. In every craft, a priest said mass. The Channel rose and fell like a roller coaster. Believe a standup paddle-boarder when he tells you—a five-foot wave can turn your stomach even when you're not at war. Fortunately for Jerry, he wasn't on the front line. Crossing through the screen smoke—a smoking curtain raised by the American Army to hide their boats—he had to clamber over the bodies of the first martyrs, bodies that had already bloated between the two waves.

*Utah Beach, Normandy, June 6, 1944. It was on this beach that Jerry
landed seventy years ago, from one of four thousand boats,
flown over by eleven thousand planes.*

The secret with landing is not to land first. The role of the first landers is to die, to ease the passage of those coming after them. On the night of June 6, an American officer told his soldiers: "Don't worry if all the first wave of you are killed. We shall simply pass over your bodies with more and more men." Some American pilots had engraved the motto of Roman gladiators on their planes: "*Morituri te salutant.*" ("Those who are about to die salute you.") Other soldiers wore Native American war paint on their cheeks or shaved their heads. The officer who designated those who would make up the first wave knew that he was sending them to their deaths. It went a little better once the first German batteries had been roasted by flamethrowers, carried by young, war-crazed dope-heads, high on Benzedrine and Methedrine (amphetamines supposedly prescribed to treat asthmatics, but in reality to amp up the G.I.s). You advance quicker when you're walking over cadavers, and at least a dead soldier can't be a land mine. Some of the G.I.s jumped from dead body to dead body like young goats hopping from rock to rock. Some bodies were naked, stripped by the blast of the explosion. Sometimes bodies shuddered beneath their boots—good thing too, that way the stretcher bearers could be alerted. There was tons of abandoned equipment everywhere—Jeeps and tanks underwater, overturned boats, sunken trucks, their loads discharged: boxes of boot polish, piles of unusable shells and rifles, razors, toothbrushes, shoes, Bibles, pants, radios, cigarettes, packets of Band-Aids...and lots of oranges, floating in the waves. One of my mother's friends lived close to Sainte-Marie-du-Mont. Like many other curious people,

he went the day after to the beach where Salinger landed. He told my mother the water was still red. Like Moses, Salinger had crossed the Red Sea.

I walk on this beach at low tide, seven decades after the blood-bath. Earlier, I went to the cemetery to gather my thoughts in front of the white crosses. The Americans landed on this beach at low tide, which surprised the Germans. That left them six hundred feet to cross—three hundred in water, three hundred on the sand. The longest six hundred feet. Two whole minutes exposed to gunfire. In this war, men were logs, casualties. But relatively few (196) were killed on Utah Beach on the sixth of June, thanks to effective bombing of the blockhouses, the sabotage carried out by parachutists in

the night, and above all the amphibious Sherman tanks, sur-rounded by a skirt of floating rubber like a fat, black buoy (at Omaha they sank because of the swell). The Shermans were elephants whose trunks spat molten metal. They surfed to the sand and disemboweled the concrete blockhouses filled with blond machine-gunners drugged up on Pervitin or Isophan, washed down with schnapps—the doping that allowed the Blitzkrieg. This was also a war of amphetamines and speed. (Russian sailors used the "Baltic cocktail"—a shot of vodka mixed with a gram of pure cocaine transformed them into army robots, drunk on violence, never tiring, and oblivious to the bullets.) Speed suppresses hunger and sleep, but in high doses can make you crazy, paranoid, and depressive, even sui-cidal. Hitler, who took cocaine from Dr. Theodor Morell as an eyewash, but also as injections, knew one thing. You snooze, you lose. You had to stay awake longer than the enemy, hurt him at the moment he relaxed. Jerry quickly understood that in this war, it was the insomniacs who survived.

Salinger had spent two and a half years waiting for this moment, and now he wanted to push back the date. "Can someone postpone D-Day a while, please?" Yet from January 1942 to June 1944, he'd had the time to get prepared. He practiced everything thousands of times—hitting the ground, covering his partner, camouflage, throwing a gre-nade, approaching the blockhouse, determining the origin of enemy gunfire, saving the wounded, fanning out, and watching the ground to avoid mortar holes and antiperson-nel mines. The result? Under machine-gun fire it's every man for himself. One young guy has his belly torn open. Another is looking for his right hand. An idiot laughs because he got through unscathed and then explodes a second later. A kid gets poked in the eye by a severed thumb. Those not praying aloud are drunk. One of the crafts rolls over a mine, and the men are thrown in the air by the dozen (thirty-nine dead of the sixty on board). The water is red, the waves are red, fish die in the hundreds, the beach is covered in them, between the bodies and the rivulets of fresh blood. And the noise is incessant: the whistling of rockets, the salvos of automatic weapons, sand in the eyes, shell explosions that burst eardrums (they had to wear their helmets loose, otherwise the vibrations from the ground could cause the strap to strangle them or break their necks), could someone PLEASE make this racket STOP? Until their deaths thirty or fifty years later, some veterans still woke up at night deafened by imaginary bombardments, screaming, begging the din to stop, with their wives blubbering beside them, rollers in their hair.

At the same time, six thousand miles away, Charlie Chaplin and Oona O'Neill were lunching together at their home on 1085 Summit Drive.

The mansion was huge, on the peak of a hill, flanked by a large swimming pool and a tennis court. Oona was sitting on an armchair, her legs crossed. The warm, late-afternoon breeze rustled the leaves of the palm trees. At the end of the English lawn, the Pacific Ocean stretched out.

"I know that this luxury might seem obscene," Charlie

*At the same time, six thousand miles away, Charlie Chaplin
and Oona O'Neill were lunching together at their home on
1085 Summit Drive.*

said, pointing out the wooded hills. "But if you knew the poverty I was born into, you would certainly forgive my taste for comfort."

"Oh, I know where you were born. I saw *The Kid*. The attic room, freezing in winter, where the child warms himself by the wood-burning stove, where he sleeps fully dressed. You didn't make that up, did you?"

"Oona, listen to me. I don't know how many years I have left to live, but I'm so happy to be spending them with you."

Los Angeles was at their feet (both literally and meta-phorically). Oona was the medicine that cured Charlie of his womanizing. She made all other women invisible. Her age meant that he would never see her get old. He was always surprised when he watched her. He had seen her every day, for months, yet saw her each time with the same astonish-ment, how someone stone-cold sober might react to seeing a UFO. Happiness, for a man, is when a woman sweeps all other women out of his life. Suddenly he feels so relived it's as if he's on holiday. Charlie only had to look at Oona to feel light. Beauty's one use is perhaps to push unhappiness back a little. Certain ephemeral constructions do end up lasting a long time—like the Eiffel Tower, built the year that Chaplin and Hitler were born.

Before Oona, he was governed by his desire. With her, desire was just a tiny part of the fullness he felt. Chaplin had long considered himself shipwrecked, abandoned by his alco-holic father and lunatic mother, exiled from his native land, stifled by the artificial admiration of groupies, addicted to success and glory. All men, and particularly those whose pro-fessions involve them sharing their emotions, are drowned creatures waiting for mouth-to-mouth. This is how Charlie proposed to Oona in 1943:

"I'm long past the midpoint in my life," he declared. "Once, Georges Clemenceau said..."

"Who?"

"A French politician. At the age of eighty-two, he said to his young girlfriend: 'I'll teach you how to live, and you'll teach me how to die.'"

"Not a chance!" Oona said. "I live very well, and I forbid

you to die!"

"Can I ask you three very important questions?"

"Okay."

"Do you love me for my money?"

"No, because tomorrow I could marry any old dope a hundred times richer."

"Do you love me for my fame?"

"No, because I was more famous than you the day I was born. It is possible I love you for your films...."

"That's not a problem. Fortunately, all that work served some purpose!"

Suddenly, the shadows of all the objects around the pool sharpened. A plane was crossing the sky.

"What was your third question?"

"Will you marry me?"

"But you've already been married. Three times!"

"Exactly. I refuse to end on a failure."

"All right. Now I have a question for you. Why do you want to marry me?"

"So that you don't marry Orson Welles!"

"Be serious!"

"Have you looked at yourself and then at me? This old, gray-haired dodderer has hit the jackpot! You are my prize. I deserve you...after all my years of wandering. From now on I'll never be able to pass myself off as a tramp. I'll need to change costume."

It's true that after his marriage with Oona O'Neill, Charlie Chaplin never dressed as a bum in his films, but always in a three-piece suit. Even when Monsieur Verdoux climbed the scaffold, he did so at the peak of sartorial elegance.

June 19, 1944
Cherbourg, France

Dear Oona,

I write you letters in my head, which I don't have time to write on paper, and which, therefore, you won't get to read. This one represents just a very small part that I barely had the time to jot down on this scrap. Everyone around me is younger! Nineteen, twenty, twenty-one...At twenty-five, I'm the troop's old-timer.

They held mass this morning. The chaplain dished out the body of Christ amid shells and wounded men. He made the dead take communion. I stayed back, shooting crap with Mathias from South Dakota and rolling smokes with Owens from New Jersey. He made me think of you. How's the beach at Point Pleasant doing? It occurred to me— Normandy is basically New Jersey's opposite number. In the end it's like I landed on your childhood beach, only the boardwalk has been replaced with blockhouses. When it's raining, a colored guy in my section sings the blues, which depresses everyone. I'm always asking myself: "What the fuck am I doing here?" But you've got to fight this question off, keep pushing it back, stop it getting to your legs. It's the suicidal question. You can even ask it in New York, at The Stork or anywhere else: "What the fuck am I doing here?" Think about it and you're stuck. I prefer to think about you, Oona. Your face is my religion. I'm not Buddhist, I'm Oonist. I know that I'm wasting my breath, that you're about to give birth, but I hold on to the romantic suffering because it helps me forget the physical pain and irrational fear. We don't decide to feel; we feel what we can. The heart uses whatever it has in stock, and mine is still piled high with you. You help me. Not you, but the idea of you. The idea of a pure baby girl who makes a stink about everything and sends salty kisses from across the Atlantic, backed up by a crummy barrel organ score. You weren't a woman. You were a concept: impossible love. Lost love. Wasted love. A heartbreaker who can't stop making people feel for her. You hurt everybody so much that I can't be mad at you. It's crazy how powerful you are! Your face has become the mask of God. You're his understudy, a replacement for a superior perfection, the bodily reflection of another truth. Your round forehead, your tearful gaze, your sweet voice, and your pure heart quench my thirst for holiness under the molten metal sky.

I stopped hating you as soon as I set foot on the French beach. You have to be careful where you walk. The S-mine clicks then— boom!—no more legs. Earlier, some poor kid heard that click under his boot and so couldn't move any farther. He was sobbing, paralyzed, standing trembling on top of an iron plate—like a live grenade, only flat—just waiting to tear his balls off. Although he was still alive, from that moment he could already be spoken about in the past tense. I turned round and, after the explosion, nothing was left except his combat boots, like two leather vases filled with guts. I don't know what the kid's name was. The other lousy thing is when a grenade lands at your feet. You have to pick it up, fast, and throw it back. Sometimes your arm goes with it.

It's difficult to explain what it feels like to be in the middle of this shambles. You daren't look around too much. You're afraid to get attached to this guy or that guy and then never see him again. It's a strange feeling keeping your eyes down and hunching over—not to dodge the bullets, but so you can't see what's happening. A flock of zig-zagging ostriches, that's what the landings are. Thousands of men in damp socks slaloming desperately so they don't get picked off. I never said to myself, "Let's hope they get the next guy." Never! Instead I said, "Forget me, I'm not worth being targeted. Don't look at me, I'm not interesting. I don't want to kill anyone. Don't shoot at me, and I won't shoot at you." In German, "Leave me alone" is "Lass mich allein."

I ended up reciting prayers as I ran from crater to crater over arterial geysers that painted my uniform bright red. The idea that we die randomly and survive by fluke is too humiliating. Prayer gives structure to chaos. Often a battle turns into a scrap, with helmet blows to the face. It just takes a revolver jammed with a grain of sand—and believe me, there's no shortage of sand on French beaches—and it's back to old-fashioned brawling, like in the pubs of Berlin or New York. Fists, rifle butts, kicking a man in the head when he's down, crushing his balls with stones, bayonet, or dagger thrusts to the belly.... Some madmen spice things up (cutting off tongues, noses, or ears, digging out eyes with a spoon, etc.). Why spend all those billions on logistics and munition transport if it's just going to end up like a drunkards' brawl in Times Square, with broken, bloody noses, busted eyes, teeth cracked by planks, or gun barrels to the larynx?

It's a lesson in modesty for our top generals and their Geological Survey maps. Do they even know that we took some bridges, villages, and roads with our bare hands, holding the Boches' heads under-water until they stopped wriggling? Modern warfare quickly turns medieval. They should have let us carry sabers like the Japanese. At least this scrappy war is on a human scale. You know the face of the guy you're knocking off—it's only four inches from your own and insulting you in the language of Goethe. It's unforgettable, especially when he's eighteen years old and bawling for his "Mutti." It's like a dance, lying on top of each other, screaming to give yourself courage, a gladiatorial combat in an ancient circus called Poche de Cherbourg. The French rugby players fared better than others in the hand-to-hand. They were used to jamming their fingers into enemy soldiers' eye sockets and breaking their shins and elbows. The enemy that met the rugby players from the southwest of France ended up crippled, their legs and arms useless, just wailing, dislocated trunks that had to be evacuated on stretchers, nice and clean, without anyone dying or any ammo being wasted, unless you think of a large stone pulled from a wall and smashed at full strength into a German's skull, split-ting it in two against the ground, as granite ammunition.

And two days later, we were passing through gutted villages, towns flattened by our planes and tanks, and the French were thank-ing us for caving in their roofs, despite the dead cows in the meadows, their eyes all covered in bugs, and the stink of decomposing horses and swollen corpses. And we started eating dirt again. It's not a met-aphor: In the Normandy farmland, the Panzer shells sent dirt flying into the air, literally, and when it fell back down, you breathed it in and chewed it up. You swallowed a dirt steak. I've eaten a whole load of Normandy. France tastes like ashes and dust, with a hint of *cow dung, but above all it tastes of broken flint (the shells shatter the rocks and it smells of split stones; scree showers down on our backs... it's a stoning!), except when it rains. Then France stinks of cold mud. Rain makes the war soft, an iron rain, underwater, and the molten sky unleashes an ocean of metal on our backs. Bombs are easy: When you hear the whistle, you've gotta hit the ground and wait for the explosion. If you're not mushed up, don't lift your head up right after the bang. There'll be flying shards for another two seconds yet. I'm tired, but it's impossible to shut your eyes and not get killed. If you sleep, you're dead.*

The chance that I'll make it out of here gets smaller every day. You should play the lottery with my birthday: For now, I'm charmed.

Your fan,

Jerome

What French People Aren't Told About the Normandy Landings (not in high school, *The Longest Day,* or *Saving Private Ryan*):

—A large majority of soldiers were drugged or drunk (just as in 1914).

—Many of them pissed themselves with fear or shit their pants, which explains the pestilential odor.

—There were a number of rapes in the liberated villages. The American Army (like the German Army) had promised its soldiers that France was the whorehouse of Europe. Soldiers with STDs filled the infirmaries; twenty-nine American soldiers were summarily tried and executed for rape between June 1944 and June 1945 (among them, twenty-five black G.I.s, victims of as much racism from the French as from the Americans).

—German soldiers' wives shot at the American troops.

—As a result, French civilians, taken for snipers, were arrested and sometimes executed by American soldiers.

—Many young French women prostituted themselves for a hunk of bread, a lump of soap, a pack of Lucky Strikes, a Hershey's bar, or even for chewing gum.

—Hundreds of German soldiers were wiped out, even though they were leaving their bunkers with their hands raised. Others were offered cigarettes or chocolate in exchange for their surrender.

—Some soldiers robbed the dead bodies, for example ripping out gold teeth with a bayonet. Sometimes the Boche were still alive when their gums were slashed open.

—Some fanatic Germans raised the white flag as if to surrender, then suddenly shot as they cried *"Heil Hitler!"*

before being sliced to bits. Many of them committed suicide in their bunkers just like the Japanese.

—In the weeks following the landings, German reinforcements were made up of blubbering adolescents between thirteen and seventeen years old. Some of them were beaten to death by the French.

—Desertion was rare because the Wehrmacht punished it by death, but it was much more common in the U.S. Army, which only executed one deserting soldier (Eddie Slovik, who refused to fight in Hürtgen Forest).

—There were around fifty thousand black soldiers in the American Army. Nicknamed the "segregated," they were forbidden from parading down the Champs-Élysées in order to "whitewash" the army's image. In this war against racism, the high-ranking U.S. officers behaved like members of the Ku Klux Klan. "Negroes" were accused of all misdemeanors and were treated much more harshly than whites at the court-martial (96 executions for murder or rape). General Leclerc's 2nd Armored Division was also "whitewashed" at the Americans' request, who didn't want to see Paris liberated by a single black man. (Charles de Gaulle conceded—none of the African soldiers who participated in the fighting were allowed to enter the capital on August 25, 1944.)

—There were two hundred concentration camps in France. Why do we only speak of Drancy, when there was also Saint-Denis, Compiègne, Moulins, Romainville, Fresnes, Vichy...? Tens of thousands of scrawny prisoners were liberated by the Allies on French territory. Six hundred thousand people were detained in these "internment camps":

Jews, resistants, gypsies, Spanish refugees, "enemy civilians," Communists.... Besides Struthof (the only Nazi camp), all the others were "managed" by the French. Tens of thousands of French people worked as camp guards, in the barracks, in the manors, the sanatoriums, or the

shacks constructed by prisoners. The conditions of detention were very hard: cold in winter, hot in summer, collective open-air latrines, rats, lice, cockroaches, fleas, all kinds of epidemics, bad treatment, and nobody had enough to eat. The prisoners fought over potato peelings

President Roosevelt was warned about the extermination of the Jews by Jan Karski at the end of 1942.

or cabbage cores. Sometimes a child's meal was a bucket full of chicken bones already chewed by dogs.

—Warned about the extermination of the Jews by Jan Karski at the end of 1942 (as well as by photos of the Warsaw ghetto in *Life*), President Roosevelt seriously considered an invasion in the spring of 1943. By deferring it a year and three months, he didn't put a stop to the Nazi death machine until April 1945. According to Raul Hilberg, around 1.3 million Jews were murdered during this period (spring 1943–spring 1945).

—From autumn 1943, imprecisely targeting munitions factories, bridges, railway lines, and ports, American B-17 and

B-24 bombers ravaged Normandy. The list of flattened towns and villages is too long to include here. The number of French civilians killed fluctuates between twenty thousand and fifty thousand, depending on the historian, two or three times greater than the number killed during the Blitz on London (which lasted eight months). Sixty-five percent of destruction during World War II in France took place during the liberation of the country (June–August 1944) compared with only 20 percent during the Battle of France (May–June 1940). Three thousand French civilians were killed during the first two days of the invasion, the same number as American casualties. One example among many: Caen was bombed from June 6 until July 19, 1944. Seventy-five percent of the town was destroyed. Between three thousand and fifteen thousand people were killed. In *Overlord,* Max Hastings argues that the bombing of Caen was one of the most useless air attacks of the war. This subject has been taboo in France because collateral damage was one of the arguments used by the Nazis and the Vichy regime against "the American invasion." When a liberating soldier enters a house with a gun in his hand, even if he comes in peace and is welcomed with a smile, lauded, and kissed, he still retains an absolute power with the risk he will abuse it absolutely. When the American Army enters a French town occupied by the Germans for the previous four years, nobody can stop it; there are no longer any laws. Even if the soldiers are spreading freedom and democracy, they are still "invading" (a term used by American generals) a country they consider—fairly, it has to be said—riddled with the Nazi ideology, a country that lost the war, a place of poverty and the black market, of prostitution and collaborations....Thefts, fights, accidents, rapes, and even murders were, for the most part, left unpunished. Seventy years later, the infinite, steadfast, and eternal gratitude that my country owes to the Allied troops won't prevent me from staring the excesses of the invasion in the eye: If you take two million men and dump them in a humiliated, dirty, poverty-stricken, and shamefaced country, it is impossible to prevent misconduct.

It is impossible to understand war if you've never been trained to fire a rifle. Anyone who has a weapon slipped into his hands is transformed. The day I felt the strongest in my life was when I got the highest score for shooting at a fixed fifty-meter target with my FAMAS rifle. I clearly remember the force of the shot as I held my breath, lying flat, the rifle butt against my shoulder, glasses pressed to the sights. I had metamorphosed into a cold-blooded sniper. Now, picture not just a guy like me, imagining himself a killer, but a thousand, ten thousand, two million supermen whose fingers spit fire. You're beginning to understand the pleasures of war. Uniforms also change men. On the set of *The Great Dictator,* Chaplin, in his military costume, became tyrannical, irascible, and violent. As soon as he changed into the Tramp's costume, he became delicate, ethereal, and attentive. You go and explain to *übermenchen* that they're here to defend human rights and the Protestant morality. The only word in their head is *freedom*. Freedom to eat, drink, fuck, rape, steal, have fun, dance, kill, and kill again until you explode.

American soldiers mocked the French.

"These Frenchies are crazy. Where are they when they have to die for their country? You think the French would come and die for Arkansas? Can you see them landing in Miami to rescue Florida?"

Jerry defended France.

"France is the Gandhi of Europe. By accepting their defeat, they saved their population. If nobody goes to war, nobody dies, man. Think about it. If nobody shoots, problem solved."

Oona is lying in her one-piece swimsuit on a sun lounger, her feet dangling in the water of the swimming pool. Her nails are manicured, her blow-dried black hair under a wide-brimmed hat, black also. Jerry is depressed by the howls of wounded animals, the whinnying of crippled horses, the lowing of disemboweled cows.... He is relieved when a charitable comrade shuts them up with a bullet. Oona waltzes with her mother in the gray living room. Agnes's novel *The Road Is Before Us* (initially called *Tourist Strip*) had good reviews in *The New York Times* and *The New Yorker.* Jerry crawls through brambles, crushed by his backpack. Oona and Charlie go into Musso & Frank, the maître d' escorts them to their box, and they nod at the stars

seated at neighboring tables. Jerry sleeps as he marches, his hand on the shoulder of the G.I. in front of him. On his tennis court, Charlie Chaplin shows Oona how to throw the ball higher to improve her serve. Jerry watches the parachutists float down from the sky like green lampshades. Some of them are dead before they hit the ground. Oona listens to the radio as she finishes her cupcake. Drenched, exhausted, full of cold, Jerry has blisters on his toes. One night, in New York, at La Vie Parisienne cabaret, at Marlene Dietrich's request, the orchestra plays "La Marseillaise" in honor of the French Resistance. Oona and Charlie stand at attention.

9
THE RITZ HOTEL, AUGUST 26, 1944

"Don't ever kid yourself about loving someone. It is just that most people are not lucky enough ever to have it. You never had it before, and now you have it. What you have with Maria, whether it lasts just through today and a part of tomorrow, or whether it lasts for a long life, is the most important thing that can happen to a human being. There will always be people who say it does not exist because they cannot have it. But I tell you it is true and that you have it, and that you are lucky even if you die tomorrow."

Ernest Hemingway,

For Whom the Bell Tolls, 1940

Jerry is twenty-five now, and a sergeant. Of the 3,080 men from the 12th Infantry who landed in Normandy, two-thirds are already dead. The figures speak for themselves: Of 155 officers, 118 died between the 6th and the 30th of June 1944. His regiment is the first to enter Paris on the 25th of August via the Porte d'Italie. He's swamped by the jubilant flower-hurling crowd. On the Avenue Raymond-Poincaré, a young girl gives Jerry a bottle of red wine that she has been hiding these past four years. Farther on, a woman holds out her baby for him to kiss...then pushes her great-grandmother at him too! He's covered with tears of joy.

Salinger had no idea what the war would do to him. His work, as a counterespionage officer, involved studying aerial photographs, scanning telephone transcripts, translating German radio messages, and interrogating prisoners. In times of war, counterespionage officers are no James Bonds; they're researchers who have to synthesize all the data so they can warn the troops, as quickly as possible, what to expect the following day: where the machine guns are, the

enemy's weak spots, the Germans' plans. Jerry speaks French and German, making him indispensable. As they're advancing through Paris, his squad flushes out a Nazi collaborator, but the mob seizes him and beats him to death in front of them. The Frenchman's head is busted "like a flowerpot." There's a similar scene in *For Whom the Bell Tolls*. Jerry is fascinated by Hemingway. Deep down, the reason he signed up for this hell was to become Hemingway.

Salinger has heard that America's most famous war correspondent is holed up at the Ritz. As a budding writer, there's nothing he wants more than to meet his master. As cell phones don't exist, he decides just to chance it. He borrows a Jeep, charges to the Ritz on the Place Vendôme, and at the front desk asks for *Monsieur* Ernest Hemingway. The inundated receptionist replies that *Mister* Hemingway is in the bar. The mustached one is swaggering about, Bordeaux in hand, surrounded by a court of soldiers. He's claiming to have liberated the palace![7]

To his great surprise, when Jerry introduces himself with "my name is Salinger, Jerome Salinger," Hemingway greets him like an old colleague and invites him to sit at his table in the bar that will one day bear his name. Dressed in shirtsleeves and dirty army slacks, sporting a mustache, salt-and-pepper crew cut, and the beginnings of a belly, Hemingway is accompanied by a resistance fighter nicknamed Marceau and a young American. He sends one article per month to *Collier's,* which published Salinger's story "The Hang of It" in its July 1941 issue. Hemingway recognizes Salinger from

---

7. The truth is a little different. When Ernest Hemingway arrived in the Ritz lobby, the Germans had already abandoned the hotel. He was welcomed by the manager, who was screaming, "We saved the Cheval Blanc!" To which Hemingway replied, "Well, go and get it!" before methodically downing the wine.

his photo in *Esquire* and remembers reading "The Heart of a Broken Story."

"Have you got anything new to show me?"

Salinger pulls out a recent copy of *The Saturday Evening Post,* with his story "Last Day of the Last Furlough." Hemingway reads it and applauds. The two writers order drinks and converse for two hours.

"Do you know, at least, what you came here looking for?"

"No, but I know what I've lost."

At first they keep their masks on: the great braggart writer and the young sycophantic private. This kind of deference is a classic of the literary life.

"Last Day of the Last Furlough" was published in July 1944 in *The Saturday Evening Post.* Written in England before the Normandy landings, it tells the story of John F. Gladwaller Jr., who has to return to the war, even though he'd rather stay home and read *Anna Karenina* and *The Great Gatsby.* He is visited by a big-eared soldier called Vincent Caulfield, twenty-nine years old, whose little brother, Holden, is missing in action. It's winter, not far from New York, and it's snowing. John is sledding with Matilda, his little sister, and he thinks: "I'm happier than I've ever been in my life.... Shoot me, all you sneaking Jap snipers that I've seen in the newsreels. Who cares?" Vincent Caulfield asks ten-year-old Matilda if she'll marry him. "It's no good being with civilians anymore. They don't know what we know...." With every story published, Jerry's style darkens, finding its originality and its madness.

Little by little, the drink takes effect. Jerry, who secretly prefers Fitzgerald, is pleasantly surprised by the difference between the public and private Hemingway. Hemingway

has his cracks too. Jerry speaks about this meeting in a let-ter dated September 4, 1944, addressed to his mentor Whit Burnett, the director of *Story*: "I found him softer than his prose." Compared with Fitzgerald, Hemingway was not an aggressive drunk and took a genuine interest in the budding author.

"I hoped the war would inspire a book," Jerry says. "But now I just don't want to talk about it."

"I said the same thing at your age," Ernest says. "But writ-ers who have gone to war will always write about it, even when they're not writing about it. It's already pumping through all your stories in the magazines."

"Those who came back from the First World War never stopped talking to their kids about it, so they'd know how horrible it was. But it turned them into heroes back from hell, and all that guff. And what was the result? Children who wanted to do just the same. So I swear never to talk about it to anyone. Everyone who fought this time should keep their traps shut. The war will be...our iceberg, right?"

Hemingway smiles. He likes conversing with a fellow writer; it's relaxing. He has sometimes compared his writing to an iceberg peeking above the water. It's kind of satisfying that a young greenhorn remembers it. In a writer's life, people never imagine how rare precise remarks about writing are, even in interviews, reviews, and conversations with colleagues. A young debutant making an attentive remark about your working method — this kind of anomaly happens four or five times in an artist's life, not more.

"The war is the underwater part," Jerry goes on. "What happens on the page is not even an eighth of what we've seen, right?"

"Writing doesn't mean telling everything," Ernest says. "You have to choose the killer detail."

"I try, but I don't cut enough."

"Nobody cuts enough," Hemingway says, looking at his cigarette. "Have you read the Bible? The old version, the King James. Read the Chronicles. It's a model narrative. I copied everything from there. It's absolute concision."

"In *For Whom the Bell Tolls*..." — Jerry went on, after writing "King James Bible: Chronicles" in his notebook — "...there's that image of the skull busted open like a flowerpot. I've seen a few split skulls, but they always looked more like busted melons, peeled watermelons, purplish octopuses, bubbling cauliflowers... for example, a tuft of hair turned over like a clod of earth, with egg white and strawberry jam poured into it. It's weird when a guy who has all this slop in his head is still alive and calls to you for help as he trembles, wide-eyed.... Ah, fuck it! I'm sorry."

Jerry downed his drink to hold off the need to puke. Hemingway bit off a mouthful of cheese. His hands trembled like Eugene O'Neill's (who had never gone to war, having been exempted in 1917 for health reasons). Jerry took out a white ashtray from his pack and held it out to Hemingway who, recognizing it, guffawed and stubbed out his cigar on the arrogant stork painted inside it.

"Ah, yes, the Stork. The crab there is excellent. I often thought of it in Spain, when dinner was just watery soup and an orange. We'll be back there before the winter. At least...I hope we will. The German winter is too hard. We have to finish them off before. What were we talking about again?"

"The skull that looked like a busted flowerpot."

"Ah, yes, the flowerpot blow. It was in Spain. The cadaver was a few days old. The skull must have been shattered by rifle butts before the guy died. And he was bald, completely hairless, and the bone had been cracked open like an egg, except it was ocher, baked-earth orange, maybe because of decomposition and the mud. It looked like a broken flowerpot lying in the street. You know, when you're on the sidewalk and you say: *Wow, a few minutes earlier, and that would have landed right on my head.*"

"Ha! A few minutes earlier... I've been saying that almost every minute since D-Day. We spend our days dodging one thing or another. The iceberg is our survival, and the submerged part is all those who've died, all those bodies underwater."

*Salinger has heard that America's most famous war correspondent
is holed up at the Ritz. As a budding writer, there's nothing
he wants more than to meet his master.*

"You remind me of Gertrude Stein. One evening at her place she said, 'It's not what France has given you that counts, but what she hasn't taken away.' It took me a long time to get what the dear old dyke meant."

Like thousands of other Americans who landed in France in 1944, they pretended to just be passing through. Booze and black humor were the only way for them to hold things together, like ER doctors on burn wards who force themselves to joke around just so they don't roll about on the floor screaming as loudly as their patients. The hotel was crawling with people. Suddenly democracy was reasserting itself. Everything was a shambles again. Fear had changed sides. The Germans were fleeing over the rooftops and the collabos were going to ground in the sewers. It was strange to be able to scream "Fuck Hitler!" in the street without ending up with matches under your fingernails.

"But the flowerpot. It was also so I didn't have to compare it to something alive. You see, Jerry, if you chose to compare dead bodies to animals or fruit or bloody meat, you may be precise, but it's less surprising than an object."

"Are you painting a still life?"

"Dear boy, I'm describing a still, dead guy." Hemingway turned to the waiter: "Albert, *ouvrez une autre, s'il vous plaît.* The more you want to be true, the less you give a damn about realism. It's not just about truth, it's about the effect created in the reader. That's what I'm after—a comparison that makes you start. Still, raspberry jam… that's a nice one."

"It tastes sweet. The surprise comes from the flavor."

They both burst out laughing.

"Yes! Sugar! *Plus de sucre!*"

"With bubbles! We want Coca-Cola!"

The Ritz's Swiss manager brought across a sugar bowl, panicked by these two drunkards who looked like father and son. He didn't know what Coca-Cola was. A few weeks earlier, the same man was obeying orders thrown about in German by Captain Ernst Jünger, who was dining with Coco Chanel and Sacha Guitry, and now he had to learn English, and quickly, to serve the American soldiers. Life on the Place Vendôme in the 1940s was no picnic.

"The day before yesterday," the maître d' said, "the Boche were still here, demanding cocaine and women! I said: *Messieurs,* it's time to leave, the *'Ricains* are coming, and they're going to drag you down the rue de Rivoli by your dicks attached to the fender of a car."

"Albert," Hemingway said. "Empty your cellar for us or this kid will have you locked up for spying for the enemy."

After Albert had left in a sweat, Jerry went on:

"I saw my latest busted skull just this morning. A collabo lynched right in front of us by a spontaneous mob of French people, transformed into wild animals. God knows what the kid had done to them. They cracked his skull with hammer blows like...like you crack a coconut. The strangest thing is that the guy did nothing to defend himself. He didn't scream his innocence or beg like they usually do. It was like what they were doing was just the way of things."

"He must have been waiting for his punishment these last four years," said Hemingway. "I saw a guy get a tire pump stuffed up his ass. They filled him with compressed air like he was a buoy. I've never heard a guy scream like that. He was begging them just to kill him."

"And you couldn't intervene?"

"It was too late. And what would you want me to do? Shoot into the crowd? A whole mass of people, terrorized for years, so hungry for revenge that they can take a man and turn him into a balloon?"

Jerry stared out the window as if he feared another lynching was taking place that moment on the rue Cambon.

"Tell me about Fitzgerald," Jerry said. "His death hit me hard."

"Poor Francis. His success killed him. He wasn't hardy enough; he hadn't been to war like us. Write what you want, big guy, but protect yourself. Stay armed, because things will turn violent when you publish your first book—whether it sells or not. Fitzgerald, poor old sod, he was successful from the off. That's the worst of all drugs. You always want more; it's never enough. And when success leaves you.... It wasn't Zelda who plugged Scott, it was the failure of *Gatsby*."

"He was a swell guy, right?"

"Adorable. He read French, you know. Have you read the French classics? Balzac, Flaubert, Musset? It's the height of distinction. You know what brings me down? After this war, it's over. Nobody is going to read French any more. That's how America will have won. We'll be read all over the world, and yet we'll only read ourselves. It began after the first war. Before 1915, only foreign writers were produced on Broadway. And then we turned inward, only staged Dreiser and O'Neill. That's what these wars have killed off—our curiosity."

On September 3, 1945, in a letter to the critic Malcolm Cowley, Hemingway mentions "a kid in the 4th division named Jerry Salinger" who expressed his disdain for the

war and his desire to write. He said he was impressed that Salinger's family was still sending him *The New Yorker*.

Neither man stopped writing during the war. Hemingway: "First, you have a marvelous ear and you write tenderly and lovingly without getting wet. How happy it makes me to read the stories and what a goddamn fine writer I think you are."

"Before leaving for the war," Jerry said, "I was going out with Oona O'Neill."

"The playwright's girl?"

"The very same."

Jerry couldn't stop himself flushing with pride.

"Good-looking gal. I saw her photo. A bit of a party animal, right?"

"That's what her father criticized her for. Me too."

"Hmm. I've been lucky enough to have three sons, but I wonder what it would have done to me to have a daughter. It's enough to drive you crazy. I'm sure I wouldn't want my daughter shimmying around the cabarets in front of those photographers...."

"She topped that. In 1942, after I'd left to join the army, Oona ditched me to marry Charlie Chaplin."

"Charlie Chaplin? Of course, how stupid of me, I read that somewhere. He's a Bolshevik, isn't he? As long as he kept his mouth shut, people loved him. The day he got mixed up in politics, everyone had it in for him."

"That should serve as a lesson. An artist is always better off remaining silent."

"Damn right, Jerry. Open your eyes. Oona chose security. And you should follow her lead. Give up on all that love-hate business, particularly if you have books to write. I should have done that at your age."

"Do you know Lamartine?"

"No."

Salinger tells him about *Graziella*:

"It's a short novel about love that I found at a farmhouse in Normandy. When he was eighteen, Lamartine fell in love with an Italian fisherman's daughter, a sixteen-year-old brunette with 'large oval eyes, the color wavering between dark black and sea blue.' Unfortunately, her parents forced the kid to flee Naples, to put some distance between him and the chances of any misalliance."

"I imagine he comes right back though, right?"

"No, it's just a memory he can never shake off. Twelve years later he comes back to Naples and looks for Graziella everywhere. In the end, he finds her tomb. She died of grief a few days after he left. Lamartine wrote the book when he was sixty."

An angel passes overhead. You can guess its Neapolitan Christian name.

"Every writer has to have his heart broken once," Hemingway says. "And the earlier the better, otherwise he's a charlatan. Writers need their own original, half-assed love to act as a revelation. Then they need to marry a kindly spouse who will stop them fucking everything up."

"Lamartine didn't love Graziella, otherwise he wouldn't have left her."

"Or maybe he wanted to set himself free?"

"And when he realized his mistake, it was already too late."

"Don't worry, Jerry. It's just a novel, an old, forgotten French novel."

Ernest boomed with laughter and poured more drinks. Newfound liberty had transformed the Ritz into an attraction park.

"You know," Jerry said. "I've been thinking about your books a lot these last two months. You've said everything there is to say about war. I love *A Farewell to Arms* because you managed to write a love story that is also a war epic. Mixing those two is tough."

"Homer had the idea first."

"Although, if you'll allow me to say so, there's one thing you didn't dare describe."

"And what's that?"

"The beauty of war. The orange and mauve clouds thrown up by the bombs, the wrecked landscapes, the burnt-out ruins in the fields, all that superb desolation, destroyed villages, the reds and yellows of the fires, the powerful far-off explosions that are like enormous fireworks on the horizon, the lunar craters... I know it's hard to accept, but war is gorgeous, don't you think?"

"I described the artillery flashes that looked like storms and the mountains of purple smoke over Italy, but you're right, I have difficulty finding the war aesthetically beautiful. I find it pretty, at least. I wasn't forced to come back, after all.... God knows I hate the war, and yet here I am, again. Something is always happening. Life is so intense, the soldier is never bored. He suffers, he's cold, he dies. No respite. And during rest hours, he drinks, he sleeps, he remembers, and he cries."

"I don't know how I'm going to be able to go back to normal life."

"That's the hardest thing. It's not the horror, so dear to old Kurtz, that stops you from living, but ordinary life, devoid of threat and risk. It's survivor's pain, and nobody can share that with you. Have you heard of Saint Teresa of Ávila?"

"No."

"She spent her life in a Spanish convent in the sixteenth century at the time America was being discovered. She wrote: 'The world is on fire.' You should get to work on a novel, my boy. Move on to something serious."

"You don't think short stories are serious?"

"They're very serious, and even more difficult, and yours are very good. But it's like boxing. People are only interested in the heavyweights."

"The world is on fire." Jerry will repeat this as he advances through Europe, the smoke pricking his eyes. As he leaves the Ritz, he takes a long look at the Stork ashtray filled with Hemingway's cigar ash and hates the dirty gray stork, still swanking despite everything it has been through. And it hasn't seen anything yet.

The streets of Beverly Hills are unbearably clean. The cars slide along the roadways; their tires never squeal. The trees smell good, the dogs don't bark, all the residents of these acacia-lined streets seem to smile because they don't have a choice—smiling is their way of expressing their gratitude that they are here while their fellow citizens are being riddled with bullet holes at Guadalcanal or roasted by flamethrowers in the swamps of Cotentin. Some newspapers are announcing an imminent invasion of California, but people are about as afraid of that as they are of the Big One, the earthquake that's supposed to swallow Los Angeles into the Pacific. The war is far away. The newsreels projected in the movie theaters show American corpses, which are then spoken about with compassion between gimlets at Ciro's (the gimlet is half gin, half lime, the ancestor of the caipirinha).

Oona is discovering a new ability to love someone other than herself. All it takes is to meet someone who really needs you. She finally feels useful. She knows that she can help Charlie Chaplin concentrate on his work; she was brought up knowing how to run a household, to handle domestic problems as well as a socialite's diary. None of that impresses her. She takes care of the garden and the kitchen without seeing it as a degrading chore—mostly because it involves just giving orders to the domestic staff. And then she admires him, her little old, blue-eyed, gray-haired genius. He's crazy for her, can't get over the fact that such a beautiful girl is neither a slut nor a whore—something so new in the sad life of one of Hollywood's founders. Once upon a time, he had sacrificed his love life for his work. Men who only think about their work tend to marry stupid or cruel women. They are easy prey, as they don't have much time to worry about happiness.

In the beginning, before their wedding, they were forced to hide from the paparazzi because of Oona's age. They couldn't go to a restaurant or attend premieres. Most often she went to his place and didn't go back to sleep at her mother's. It was light, he was thoughtful, intimidated by their age difference, never stopped saying how grotesque this was, that he didn't deserve her. She replied with exactly the same words. They drank champagne and only stopped apologizing when they were too drunk to do so. Neither of them planned it this way. It was nobody's fault. It was chance, and they spend hours remembering their first meeting, down to the smallest detail—Mrs. Wallis's awkwardness, the stupidity of how their conversation began, the shame as he remembered how embarrassed he was, her feeling of ridiculousness over her naive questions about *The Great Dictator.* They loved retelling that first evening in real time, making the story last as long as the reality, as if to relive it, again and again, eternally. Their wedding was celebrated on the sly in Carpinteria (near Santa Barbara), just after Oona turned eighteen.

Everything that had to happen for a woman like Geraldine Chaplin to be born, in order: Irish emigration to America, Charlie's voyage to Hollywood, Eugene meeting Agnes, the wild years of silent cinema, the imprisonment of a major playwright in his internal theater, the silent tragedy of divorce when divorce didn't exist, Charlie's three failed marriages as he invented popular cinema, the Wall Street crash in 1929, Oona's frantic loneliness in Manhattan, Pearl Harbor, Jerry leaving for the war.... It took coincidences and random events. There was one chance in a billion that, together, they would create Geraldine Chaplin, who was born in Santa Monica on July 31, 1944, so that twenty years later she could act in *Doctor Zhivago* and her daughter, Oona Castilla Chaplin, could be stabbed in her pregnant belly in *Game of Thrones*.

There was one chance in a billion that they would create Geraldine Chaplin, who was born in Santa Monica on July 31, 1944, so that twenty years later she could act in Doctor Zhivago.

*The soldiers nicknamed Hürtgen Forest "the meat factory."
It was a new, frozen Verdun. This hellhole, worse than any
Vietnamese jungle, was very cold.*

The 4th division entered Hürtgen Forest on November 6, 1944, exactly five months after they landed on Utah Beach. They would remain there until February 1945. Compared with this confrontation, the battle for Normandy was a walk in the park. Situated on the border between Belgium and Germany, to the southeast of Aix-la-Chapelle, the soldiers nicknamed Hürtgen Forest "the meat factory." It was a new, frozen Verdun. This hellhole, worse than any Vietnamese jungle, was very cold. Every yard was muddy, dangerous, and deadly. There was barbed wire, land mines, buried machine-gun posts, explosive traps, very steep hills, thick and bushy vegetation, incessant rain and snow, phosphorous bombs that burned thousands alive, not including those killed by "friendly fire" (hundreds were killed by accident or human error). It was a forgotten butchery: The Germans fought like dogs, just as in 1917. They didn't have much of a choice: If they had fallen back, not only were the teenage soldiers (some as young as twelve or thirteen) hanged by the Nazis, but they were made to believe the Gestapo would massacre their families. Shots fired in the forest are doubly cruel because as the bullets ricochet off the trees, they send shards of bark flying like murderous arrows. And that's without mentioning the collapsing trunks. Any wounded quickly died of cold. Cadavers were found in the early morning, turned blue and hardened by the frost.

For eight days and eight nights, Jerry doesn't sleep: He is buried, shivering, in holes filled with water, his feet turned to ice cubes. He will spend the rest of his life allergic to the cold. The frozen wind is never forgotten; it is impossible to think of anything else. The German mortars were burying the G.I.s alive, but they were almost relieved to find themselves blanketed in dirt, in an improvised trench, warmed by their own blood. They never took showers, wore the same shoes and underwear for months, and their battledress was so muddy and blood-soaked that it could stand up unsupported. When everything is drenched or solidified by the cold, you can kiss hygiene good-bye. Dirt becomes a kind of bark, stench a kind of armor. The Americans thought victory would come early, so no preparations had been made to help the infantrymen get through the winter (boots without fur lining, coats that never dried—soldiers fought each other over the rabbit-skin pea jackets they stole from the German cadavers). Thousands suffered from frostbite, losing fingers and toes in the forest—think Tom Thumb sowing digits so he could find his way back home. The American infirmary lacked everything: They were out of bandages and out of morphine. Every German bunker taken, surrounded by mines and barbed wire, claimed hundreds of lives for an advance of just a few feet. In Hürtgen Forest, there were huge numbers of self-mutilation cases: G.I.s shooting themselves in the hand or arm so they could be evacuated. Jerry saw one soldier ask another to break his leg between his rifle butt and a tree. The infantrymen, lying in the snow, took bullets in the head, shoulders, or thighs. Those who were hit in the shoulders or thighs were overjoyed—they were going home! Even losing a foot to a land mine was good news. Only one deserter was shot (Eddie Slovik, January 31, 1945), but how many actually fled? Numbers vary. According to historian Charles Glass, around fifty thousand American soldiers deserted their posts during the Second World War, the equivalent of ten divisions. Some

were court-martialed, but the majority are still on the run...
or died a long time ago.

The German General Freiherr von Gersdorff declared
this battle worse than anything he had seen on the Russian
front. It involved taking of the Siegfried Line, which the
French and English couldn't manage in 1940. The Phoney
War had involved waiting to be circumvented to avoid a
massacre. The defeat in 1940 delayed the job by four years,
when France delegated the sacrifice to young Americans who
crossed the ocean to be killed in one of Germany's black
forests. One thousand dead per day, the same as at Verdun.
Thirty-three thousand of 120,000 soldiers died. Today, the
battle of Hürtgen is recognized by historians as a strategic
error. The deaths were useless, as the German Army could
have been circumvented to the south, avoiding the deadly
forest. Those responsible for this gratuitous massacre were
General Omar Bradley and General James Hodges. They
thought the Germans had to be dislodged from the forest
so they could cross the Rhine. The decision to take the forest was, according to the American historian Stephen E.
Ambrose, "grossly, even criminally stupid." Werner Kleeman,
one of Jerry's comrades in arms, called it a "suicide mission."
And during this forgotten butchery, Paris was celebrating the
liberation.... Until the 1960s, the French spoke of the "39–
44 War." For them, the job was done. If the United States
had had the atomic bomb in winter 1944, they would have
dropped it on Berlin without the slightest hesitation.

Jerry had been lucky in Normandy, then in Cherbourg,
then in Paris, then in Germany. When you are this lucky, it is
no longer luck. If he was still alive, it was because someone,

For eight days and eight nights, Jerry doesn't sleep: He is buried, shivering, in holes filled with water, his feet turned to ice cubes.

somewhere, had decided he should write. At first, it was superstition, but now he had faith. He had to live in order to tell what he had lived through. But Jerry knew that he would never be able to. He wouldn't bear witness. He would shut up. In Salinger's work, the war is a huge omission. But here, in Hürtgen Forest, he had become indebted. All around him, soldiers were getting wounded, going crazy from the pain, repeating two contradictory sentences over and over:

"Stop killing us! Stop killing us!"

"Kill mc! Kill me!"

Jerry would never leave the forest. Later on, he'd chose to live in a different one, near Cornish.

When he sees Hemingway again in December 1944, in Zweifall, he's no longer the young, dashing, and ambitious man from Paris that past August. In a little brick house on the edge of the forest, painted with the letters P.R.O. (Public Relations Office), they drink champagne from aluminum mess tins in silence.

"We were better off at the Ritz," Jerry says.

"Hell, yeah!" says Ernest.

"Have you written anything here?"

"An article, a couple of dialogues. Nothing more. That's my method, right? The less I write, the better I feel."

He's coughing a lot. Hemingway doesn't know it yet, but he has caught pneumonia. The champagne was frozen solid; they warm it in their hands like a toddy.

"Just action and dialogue, like in the movies."

"That's your secret. And a bit of scenery from time to time. Is that allowed?"

"OK, but quickly though."

In the distance they hear bombs exploding like a

thunderstorm. They are less cocky now than in the summer. For the rest of their lives, every storm will remind them of the mortar shells. Through the window, the snow looks like cornflakes falling from the sky.

"Would you mind if I asked you to shoot me in the arm with your Colt 45?" Jerry asks.

"If you want something done right, you have to do it yourself," Ernest replies, holding out his handgun, which he is gripping by the barrel, directed toward himself.

The story, according to which Hemingway whipped out a Nazi Luger to shoot a live chicken bellowing "Jesus, he has a hell of a talent!" is not backed up by any witnesses.

Germany would surrender five months later. Hemingway

disposed of himself sixteen years after that.

"Leave him be," Ernest says to the soldiers aiming their pistols at Jerry, about to take him on his word. "He's Jewish, which means he's funnier than you, even if he laughs less."

Jerry doesn't know how to aim. His rifle is always wavering, and he systematically misses targets six feet away. Oona prunes white rose bushes in the park with red secateurs. Jerry digs a ditch in the mud in the freezing rain. Oona, sporting a white skirt, loses a set of tennis 6–1 on the garden court. Jerry lies on his front on a rock, to steal an hour of shut-eye somewhere that isn't wet. Oona feels a few little kicks in her swollen belly. Jerry struggles to reload his rifle with frozen fingers. Oona orders strawberries and raspberries from the grocery, as well as vanilla ice cream. Jerry checks to see that his vial of morphine and hypodermic needle are still in the pocket of his pea jacket. Oona plays badminton on Santa Monica beach. Jerry listens to the explosion of bomb after bomb after bomb, always thinking that the next one will have his name on it. Oona hears on California radio that the war is almost over. Jerry writes *The Catcher in the Rye* listening to *The Lucky Strike Program* (Frank Sinatra, Glenn Miller). Charlie orders kidneys at Ciro's. Sometimes Jerry envies those who have died—being dead is much more quiet than being alive. Oona and Charlie dine at the Trocadero, at the Parisien, at Allah's Garden. Jerry shares a bottle of Calvados with three comrades, two of whom will be killed in combat that very day. Oona breathes the aroma of eucalyptus. Jerry receives a parcel from his mother with woolen socks she knitted. "After that, I was the only soldier I knew with dry feet."

April 27, 1945—The liberation of the Kaufering IV concentration camp, near Dachau. At first, Jerry thought it was a stack of white wood. But the branches of dead wood have feet, hands, and gray heads. As he approaches, he realizes they are human bones. Forty-five hundred bodies are piled up on the grounds, against the shacks, in the ditches, all around him. Suddenly, under four layers of cadavers, he

Dear Oona,
For the rest of my life I'll be ashamed about not entering the camps sooner.
Even though I know I wasn't actually guilty, I will never be able to let
myself off the hook.

sees one blink. Others emit guttural noises to allow themselves to be found under the scores of dead bodies. The pile stirs again.

As a counterespionage officer, Jerry is one of the first in to the "Krankenlager." Kaufering was an annex of Dachau reserved for the infirm—in reality an extermination camp, for the sick were neither treated nor fed in their unheated shacks. The day before the Americans arrived, three thousand prisoners were executed by machine-gun fire or by blows from iron bars and axes for those too weak to walk.

A shack full of sick people was locked and set on fire. The first G.I.s to arrive opened the hangar to find hundreds of bodies burned to a cinder. Jerry approaches the barbwire fence and sees a handful of prisoners, their skin hanging from their bones, adults weighing sixty-five pounds, with legs like chopsticks and bulging eyes. Their faces are so thin that their cheekbones stick out like horns. They lower their heads as a sign of submission, not daring to look their liberators in the eye. According to several witnesses cited in Shane Salerno's *Salinger,* the first soldiers to arrive there collapsed to the ground in floods of tears. Others threw up, then handed their rifles to survivors so that they could execute the rare guards to be captured (some SS had dressed up as prisoners, but were easily recognizable for their good health). Other soldiers drew back in fear when the survivors tried to hug or touch them. Some of the walking skeletons tried to clap, but their scraggy hands met without producing the slightest noise.

"You never really get the smell of burning flesh out of your nose entirely, no matter how long you live," Jerry said to his daughter Margaret. The smell of cooked bodies is harsh, sweet, sickly, it clings to the nostrils, gets under the skin, can never be washed away. Jerry will be forever impregnated with the stench of human meat, of cooked blood, the aroma of roasted children. Let's not beat around the bush: A death camp stinks of shit, of blood, of rot, of piss, of vomit, of human grease, for miles around. The residents of nearby villages who claimed not to know what was happening were probably suffering from a rare form of collective anosmia.

Kaufering
April 30, 1945

Dear Oona,

For the rest of my life I'll be ashamed about not entering the camps sooner. Even though I know I wasn't actually guilty, I will never be able to let myself off the hook. When interrogating the prisoners, I came to understand that there is no difference between the Germans and us. A combination of factors led to this unprecedented spectacle, and I am one of the causes, even if a distant one, of this degradation. Anyone alive at the moment, near or far, is an accomplice, whether willfully or not. It was historical reasons that drove humanity into hell. I'm writing this, vainly, to clear my name. The prisoners asked for food. We gave them our concentrated rations, and several dozen survivors died the next day. We could have bombed the railway tracks, the watchtowers, the ovens. Why did it take us three years to get here? A telegram from the Red Army let us know that Hitler had blown his brains out in a Berlin bunker. I refuse to be found blameless for this crime. We must all pay for this anomaly in our species. One day or another, we'll all have to pay for what happened here.

For a joke I grew the same mustache as Hitler and Chaplin, but I shaved it off yesterday.

I'm happy to know you're sheltered from this whole goddamn mess.

Jerome

In 2014, songs about heroism were played all day long on the radio: College's "A Real Hero" (from the *Drive* soundtrack), Chad Kroeger's "Hero" (from *Spider-Man*), Megadeth's "The World Needs a Hero," Regina Spektor's "Hero," Beyoncé's "Save the Hero," Mariah Carey's "Hero," Enrique Iglesias's "Hero," not to mention the classics—David Bowie's "Heroes," the Beach Boys' "Heroes and Villains." Teenagers flock to blockbuster movies produced by Marvel or DC Comics: *Superman, Batman, Spider-Man, Iron Man, Watchmen, X-Men, The Avengers, Captain America, Wolverine, Hulk, Deadpool,* etc. What difference is there between this desire for power and the Nietzschean fascination with the superman? Between *Storm of Steel* and *Man of Steel?* Between Wagner's Valkyries and Marvel's Thor? When the American movie industry is not spending its time imagining all manner of supermen, it is spending millions of dollars telling us stories about the end of the world. The apocalypse is Hollywood's bread and butter.

There comes a moment, in certain countries at certain times, when people seem to be expecting an important and tragic event that will allow for the resolution of all the world's problems. These periods are generally known as "prewar."

The world is ready for the next one. A new world conflict would wipe out public debt, relaunch economic growth, reduce overpopulation. The spoiled and forgetful kids in rich countries find themselves unconsciously hoping that a new cataclysm will free up space for survivors. They want to leave a mark. They dream, without acknowledging it, that History has not ended. They are looking for a new utopia, for new divisions. They are looking for a new enemy to slaughter. They would like to be traumatized by something other than *Saw* on YouTube. The youth of 2014 is in mourning for tragic choices. Destruction is lacking. Previous generations bequeathed them enormous debt, mass unemployment, and a polluted planet, existential ennui, the feeling of emptiness, the globalized frustration that feeds that frightening desire known as nihilism. A desire to be useful, to fight for an ideal, to choose sides, to risk their lives, to become heroes. It is not surprising that some of them become terrorists — what is terrorism if not the only chance for antiheroes, during peacetime, to improvise a war? The longest period of calm in the history of the West is perhaps on its way out.

I'm afraid of heroes, and yet I'm writing a book about one of them.

In 1945, the war couldn't stop finishing. California was floundering in paranoia. Oona had had her fill of the interminable propaganda: JAPS OUT scrawled on banners, and all the Japanese Americans deported to desert camps, including Chaplin's butler, Frank Yonamori. And then came August 6, the day Hiroshima was bombed. Upon hearing the news, Oona spat out her tea onto the lawn. Three days later, Nagasaki was flattened in turn. The Californians were dancing in the streets, celebrating the explosion of the secret weapon that liquidated the Japanese — the American government had offered its citizens a patriotic mushroom-shaped fireworks show. Newspaper headlines celebrated the massacre. Until the Japanese surrender on

Californians were dancing in the streets, celebrating the explosion of the secret weapon that liquidated the Japanese— the American government had offered its citizens a patriotic mushroom-shaped fireworks show.

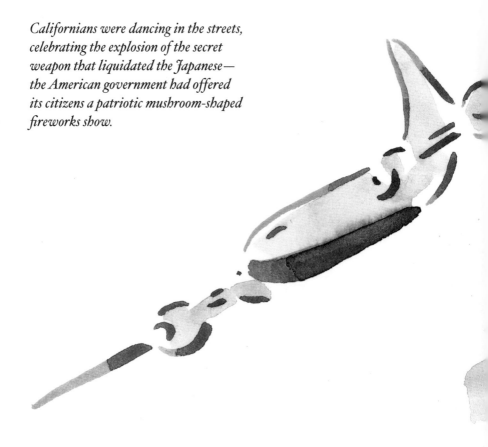

September 2, Charlie and Oona didn't leave their home. They couldn't understand their neighbors' enthusiasm. Oona felt nauseous throughout August—she was pregnant once again. From that summer of 1945, the gap separating Charlie Chaplin and Hollywood would only grow. The cinema community had forgiven him his arrests for drunk and disorderly behavior on the sidewalk of Hollywood Boulevard, his horse races with Douglas Fairbanks in front of Musso & Frank (the loser paid for lunch), and his emotional and sexual escapades, but it would never forgive him his support for the USSR during the war, or his reluctance to celebrate Hiroshima and Nagasaki, or his British immigrant bloody-mindedness, continuing to buy his clothes from Anderson & Sheppard (Savile Row, London) instead of from Americans. At his Sunday cocktail party, Charles Chaplin received Jean Renoir, Evelyn Waugh, H.G. Wells, Albert Einstein, Thomas Mann, and Bertolt

Brecht. Christopher Isherwood fell into an alcoholic coma and pissed on the living room couch. Dylan Thomas drove his car, dead drunk and with Shelley Winters beside him, across the park and right up to the tennis court. Fortunately, the racing cabriolet was stopped by the net. Chaplin had snubbed Hollywood, and Hollywood would make him pay for it. Within the space of a few years, the most popular man in America had become public enemy number one. He was accused of not being a patriot, of having supported the Communists during a meeting for the "Second Front" at Madison Square Garden on July 22, 1942 (where he, involuntarily, made the room explode with laughter by beginning his speech with "Comrades!"), and for refusing American citizenship. Even the final speech of *The Great Dictator*, those six minutes in which Chaplin spoke for the first time in a movie, delivering an idealistic, humanist, and internationalist eulogy, was considered ultraleftist! Even today, the founder of United Artists, the creator of modern cinema, the inventor of the Hollywood myth, does not have his handprint on the sidewalk in front of the Chinese Theater, even though Hugo Boss, who made uniforms for the SS, the Hitler Youth, and the Wehrmacht, has a flagship store on Rodeo Drive. Even though BMWs and Mercedes—whose engines, built by deported Jewish slaves in concentration camps, were the main force behind the Blitzkrieg—parade through the streets of Beverly Hills. I asked the doorman of the world's most famous cinema why Chaplin was absent from his sidewalk, and he replied, "Because he was a Commie!" I guess, then, it was better to be a Nazi.

Chaplin had snubbed Hollywood, and Hollywood would make him pay for it. Within the space of a few years, the most popular man in America was accused of not being a patriot, of having supported the Communists, and for refusing American citizenship.

10
POST-TRAUMATIC STRESS DISORDER

"You never saw six-feet-two of muscle and typewriter ribbon get out of a jeep and into a ditch as fast as this baby can. And I don't get out until they start bulldozing an airfield over me."

J.D. Salinger, letter to Whit Burnett

Jerry doesn't know how many weeks he's been lying in this hospital bed. What he does remember is trying to kill himself by swallowing a handful of pills, and failing. And now he's drinking German chicken broth, being pampered by nurses from Arkansas, and there are bars on the window.

The silence is doing him good. He repeats the same word all day long: Fubar. I'm fubar. Fucked Up Beyond All Recognition.

Dear Oona,

Blue pill 88 puts you to sleep for twenty-four hours. They gave me three.

The war created a strange situation. One country attacks another by surprise. It massacres with flame throwers, pillages its wealth, and moves into its homes. Another country rides to the rescue, which gives rise to the strange situation—Jim machine-guns Hans who slashes Bob who disembowels Kurt. These four kids don't know each other. Maybe if they had been introduced in a bar, they would have got along and drunk beer together. But that wasn't possible—they cut each other's arms off and will never get over it. Even if they survive their physical injuries, they'll never think of anything else except that day. Not to mention the horrible consequences lined up for the kids and grandkids of Jim, Hans, Bob, and Kurt.

The hardest thing is the noise. When I was advancing with my comrades, who dropped one after the other to pick up their severed feet, I kept repeating something, almost as a mantra: "Shut up, shut up, shut your mouth...." The goal of war is to make the cannons shut up. I didn't kill many people, but I remember one soldier whom I targeted carefully, calmly, before lightly pressing the trigger of my M1. I watched in slow motion, as if in a movie, as his head split in two when my bullet entered his right cheek. It was horribly reassuring to know that he was dead and I wasn't. The goal of war is not to make peace, but to have peace. Turn off, rub out, scratch away the smoke that has been making my eyes itch these last three years. "Smoke gets in your eyes..." Do you remember our song? Take a hot bath and wash it all off. Turn the volume down. I take ten showers a day here. As soon as I'm dry, I start again, but I'm never clean. There's always the incessant buzzing of flies. That unending background noise can drive you crazy. No more sound. No more visions. Please! If I remember only one noise from the war it'll be the whistling of bullets that sieve through men like razor blades through watermelon. It's weird: The adrenaline rush of combat first makes us hysterical, then knocks us down flat. I don't know how to explain it to you. Fear can knock you to the ground, leave you immobile, like a heart attack. Some of them here call it Shellitis... an allergy to shells! As if there is any- one who likes shells! Shellophiles—personally, I've never met any. In battle, nothing happens as planned. They say that one in four soldiers suffers psychiatric problems, although I reckon it's closer to four in four. It's just that the craziest three-quarters are the ones who seem to be doing well. We never understand what happens in the theater of operations. You've seen all the officers' maps, listened to the gener- als' briefings, followed classes in military tactics...then when you hit the battlefield it's a complete shambles and every man for himself. Patton said that the secret is to move and fire at the same time. He forgot to say you should scream too. That does you good. In the films, the soldiers are silent and graceful. In reality we howl like Vikings.

Jerry

It hurts to walk along the corridor to the latrine. He can't read. Letters don't form words, only hieroglyphs. He desperately attempts a paragraph, but his brain refuses to register anything other than the stench of roasted human meat. He has flashbacks. It only takes a slammed door or a kettle's whistle for Jerry to hear bombs exploding in his head.

Dear Poppa,

I'm writing from a General Hospital in Nurnberg. There's a notable absence of Catherine Barclays[8], is all I've got to say. I expect to get out tomorrow or the next day. Nothing was wrong with me except I've been in an almost constant state of despondency, and I thought it would be good to talk to somebody sane. They asked about my sex life (which couldn't be normaler—gracious!) and about my childhood (Normal. My mother took me to school till I was twenty-four—but you know New York streets)... I've always liked the army.

> *...*

There are very few arrests left to be made in our section. We're now picking up children under ten if their attitudes are snotty. Gotta get those ole arrest forms up to Army, gotta fatten up the Report.

> *...*

How is your novel coming? I hope you're working hard on it. Don't sell it to the movies. You're a rich guy. As Chairman of your many fan clubs, I know I speak for all the members when I say Down with Gary Cooper.

> *...*

I've written a couple more of my incestuous stories and several poems, and part of a play. If I ever get out of the army I might finish the play and invite Margaret O'Brien to play with me in it. With

8. [sic.] Catherine Barkley is the name of the heroine in *A Farewell to Arms,* a pretty nurse with whom the narrator falls in love.

a crew cut and a Max Factor dimple over my navel, I could play Holden Caulfield myself. I once gave a very sensitive performance as Raleigh in "Journey's End." Very Sensitive.

...

I'd give my right arm to get out of the army, but not on a psychiatric, this-man-is-not-fit-for-army-life ticket. I have a very sensitive novel in mind, and I won't have the author called a jerk in 1950. I am a jerk, but the wrong people mustn't know it.

I wish you'd drop me a line if you ever can manage it. Removed from the scene, is it much easier to think clearly? I mean with your work.

...

The talks I had with you here were the only hopeful minutes of the whole business.

[Genuine letter from J.D. Salinger to Ernest Hemingway, cited by Bradley R. McDuffie in *The Hemingway Review,* Spring 2011.]

Prostrate, curled up on his bed, his arms around his legs, folded to his chest in the fetal position, Jerry was unable to sleep without barbiturates for six months after the end of the war. Sometimes he cried until dawn, unable to stop. After the German surrender, he wondered if the madness was permanent crazy or just temporary. Every day was the same, and nights seemed to last twice as long. Time didn't heal; all hours were identical. He had tried to end it all—both days and nights—by mixing all the pills he could find in the ward. He never ate, was convinced he'd never smile again. He resembled the scrawny bodies he'd lifted from the floor at Dachau—a skeleton covered in creased skin, sunken eyes, devoid of everything, sans flesh, sans soul, a broken marionette, a monster, a zombie. The trend for films about the living dead dates from after the war. One can guess where American movie directors found their inspiration. The

Nazis had created monsters that ruled in favor of their racism—nobody wanted to see them; they gave you insomnia. Zombies had saved zombies created by zombies. It had nothing to do with humanity. Humanity was an obsolete concept, disqualified, soon to be replaced, in the century following, by post-humanity. Denazification was an impossible task. The Nazis had burned all traces. Public burning was their favorite sport—they even did it with their own work. How to distinguish between the war criminals and the German victims of Adolf Hitler? The bosses passed for underlings, explaining that their real bosses had all killed themselves and they had done everything they could to help the Jews. Killers wore the masks of innocents. They couldn't just gun down a whole country. They needed the Germans to rebuild Germany. World War I had led to World War II. To avoid World War II leading to World War III, they had, above all, to avoid humiliating the Germans again.

Jerry Salinger, a Jew, had seen what nobody should see. He had fought to save starving, tortured, frozen, gassed, burned Jews. That's how it was. He had to accept it: He had gone to war for these crawling skeletons. What he couldn't have imagined was that peace would not set anybody free. The massacre had gone too far; the American Army had arrived too late. Peace was useless. He often dreamed of a female skeleton screaming at him: "Thank you! Oh, thank you! But what took you so long? You landed in June, liberated Paris in August, and we were dying every day. I lost my sister in November—we were still waiting for you. My father was executed in February. Where were you? And they killed the children. Every day. And they locked a thousand people in a barn and set it alight. And they broke our teeth and put out our eyes, every day, and you never came. Never!" In his dream she collapsed in tears, hysterical. "Oh, my God, I'm hungry! What have you got on you to eat?" And he didn't know what to reply. He held out his ration. Nobody had warned them. He couldn't have guessed that he shouldn't feed them. These morbid, inadmissible thoughts ran through Jerry's head just like, much later, the Buddhist mantras and Zen koans would help him live in his voluntary reclusion in Cornish. Nobody is prepared to witness the Apocalypse, particularly at twenty-five. He didn't want to be thanked; he just wanted to forget. He was sleepy without sleep. He trembled like a leaf behind his bedroom window. And it began again. And it went on. Chemical death had given him the most meager respite. When the military doctor asked him how he felt, he always replied the same sentence: "The world is on fire."

One day, he managed to make it into the garden. He sat under a tree the whole afternoon. He let flies settle on his eyes. He saw what he didn't want to see. He heard the rumble of the panzers' tracks and the nosediving Stukas, the click of explosive mines underfoot and the whistle of bullets cleaving entrails. He envied the flies. He wanted to be the fly resting on his hand, washing, rubbing its legs together, flying away, then coming back to land on his face. He regretted killing so many of them when he was a kid. What does a traumatized soldier look like? A great dazed oaf asking forgiveness from a fly.

The psychological erosion of Jerry Salinger, fantasist, would never heal. His anxiety would never vanish. One doesn't recover from post-traumatic stress disorder. The suicide of Seymour Glass in "A Perfect Day for Bananafish" is undoubtedly autobiographical. From May 1945, Jerry—or J.D. as he then called himself—had become one of the living dead. Or rather, like a lot of soldiers suffering from veterans' syndrome often declare—he's not dead, but neither is he one of the living. His reclusion begins here. His isolation was not a dandy's choice but collateral damage from the liberation of France and Germany. Salinger was a romantic in 1940, a spy in 1943, bipolar in 1945, and then agoraphobic until his death.

In "Soft-Boiled Sergeant," a short story published in April 1944, one year before his suicide attempt, Salinger criticizes cinema for showing soldiers dying happily: *You see a lot of real handsome guys always getting shot pretty neat, right where it don't spoil their looks none, and they always got plenty of time, before they croak, to give their love to some doll back home, with who, in the beginning of the pitcher, they had a real serious misunderstanding about what dress she should ought to wear to the college dance. Or the guy that's croaking nice and slow has got plenty of time to hand over the papers he captured off the enemy general or to explain what the whole pitcher's about in the first place. And meantime, all the other real handsome guys, his buddies, got plenty of time to watch the handsomest guy croak. Then you don't see no more, except you hear some guy with a bugle handy take time off to blow "Taps." Then you see the dead guy's home town, and around a million people, including the mayor and the dead guy's folks and his doll, and maybe the President, all around the guy's box, making speeches and wearing medals and looking spiffier in mourning duds than most folks so all dolled up for a party.*

In reality, the great close-up speech should be replaced by

the screams of a polecat in the background. The only message soldiers leave behind is "Help me! Mommy!" And as for national homage—you have to make do with a standard letter handed to you by an officer with an undertaker's face. What causes a veteran's trauma isn't the indifference or the lack of recognition, but the fact that life goes on. Back in New York, Jerry crumbled when he saw the fat doorman of his building walking his dog every day just like he had done before the war. People were just getting on with their lives— eating their breakfast, buying their groceries at the deli, taking their little bow-wows for a walk around the block. The gap: That is the main cause of a veteran's depression. Indeed, it was for this very life that they had fought. But the apparition of the old imperturbable doorman was enough for Jerry to spend a good part of the night curled up in his garage, his head in his hands, unable to stop hiccupping.

In "Soft-Boiled Sergeant," a young officer called Burke takes another soldier to the cinema to see a Charlie Chaplin film. The sergeant has just learned that his girlfriend has married someone else. And, what do you know, he sees his ex in the cinema, a pretty redhead sitting with her new lover. The film begins, but the sergeant gets up in the middle of it to leave. He says to the other: *"Stay and see it, Mac. I'll be outside."*

When he comes out after the film, the two of them have this short conversation:

"What's the matter, Mr. Burke? Don't you like Charlie Chaplin none?" My sides was hurting from laughing at Charlie.

Burke says, "He's all right. Only I don't like when funny-looking little guys always get chased by big guys. Never getting no girl, like. For keeps like."

Sergeant Burke ends up getting killed by a Japanese Zero at Pearl Harbor.

An interesting hypothesis, even if rather twisted, is that Charlie Chaplin—who had already stolen Oona—was, in fact, the true inventor of the eternal and tortured adolescent. All Salinger did was co-opt the figure of the "Tramp." *The Catcher in the Rye* is a successor to *City Lights,* in which the bowler hat is replaced by the baseball cap. The purity of children and the corruption of adults—Chaplin's films speak of nothing else. He initiated the movement. As for the bourgeois caricature, Balzac, Flaubert, and Zola had already laid the groundwork. An American novel had finished it off: *Babbitt,* by Sinclair Lewis, in 1922. All that was left to do was take the figure of the romantic and depressive adolescent, a figure already present in Goethe and Musset. Holden Caulfield is a mix of Chaplin and Octave from *Confession of a Child of the Century.*

After the war, between 1946 and 1951 (the year *Catcher* was published), J.D. Salinger goes to listen to Billie Holiday, Art Tatum, and Charlie Parker in jazz clubs like the Blue Angel on 52nd Street between Sixth Avenue and Broadway. He also sometimes goes back to the Stork Club. One evening he sees Humphrey Bogart accompanied by a giant plush panda that he introduces to everyone as his fiancée. A girl tries to steal his panda, and a fight breaks out[9]. Perhaps Jerry saw Oona again. She sometimes dined with Chaplin at the Stork, always at the same table as before the war. I don't think they would have spoken; Chaplin was intensely jealous. But I imagine Jerry alone at the bar, mulling over his past and his loneliness, listening to the music and laughter, watching the fights and the open-mouthed embraces. Jerry in the big room, Oona

9. Lauren Bacall tells this story in her memoir, *By Myself,* Ballantine, 1984.

and her husband in the Cub Room, each a part of their own world. The Stork stayed open throughout 1944 and 1945, the war's longest year. I imagine Salinger laughing too loudly, downing whiskey, and speaking to himself. I see the barman asking him if there's a problem:

"Hey! Drink one with me," Jerry says. "I beat Hitler, for God's sake!"

"No thanks," the barman replies.

"No, you're gonna have one, you slacker!" And Jerry throws his drink in the barman's face.

"Lick your cheeks to my fucking health! Otherwise I'll cut you open to see what you've got in your belly."

Jerry is carried outside by the doormen, kicked out of the Stork Club. Beaten and drunk like Joaquin Phoenix at the beginning of *The Master.*

"That was my table! Number six! That was my place.... Bastard!"

This is all highly likely. If Salinger left New York, it is probably because he could no longer get in anywhere. Adolf Hitler suffered the same traumatized veteran bitterness in 1919. Demobbed and defeated, frustrated and idle, a beaten loser, Jerry fled so as not to become a dictator.

New York, December 1947

Dear Oona,

I'm happy for you. You looked radiant yesterday night at table six of the Stork. Your golden dress was like yellow champagne cascading over your marble shoulders. I thought I'd be able to come home and pick up a normal life again, but I just can't do it. I'm no longer part of the American Dream; I can't just slide back into society and order crêpes suzette under starry skies. I just feel imprisoned, isolated, depressed—remember how that was our favorite word?

Suddenly, the rumbling stopped, and everything was finished. I had difficulty getting used to silence. I don't know how to do the groceries without hitting the ground to hide. I don't know how to talk to people without pulling a pin from a grenade and blowing their brains out. They don't realize it, and I scare them with my haggard eyes. I don't know how to walk in the street without jumping at the slightest noise and diving behind the trash cans for shelter. Civilian life is like a war to stay normal. I sense that the good citizens are annoyed that I'm no longer able to be light. They rush around, useless, late for the office. But I don't ask better for myself—I dream of going to the office, or listening to jazz all day without remembering. I can now only bear talking to very young girls or very old trees.

Every night I dream I am back there. With the prisoners' hands reaching out and us giving them too much to eat. Their stomachs swelling and their ribcages expanding for all to see. They were crying, but no tears came out of their eyes. It was that separation that was so awful—them crying with joy, us with disgust. Every morning I'm happy to wake up, but every night I'm afraid to go to sleep because I know that I'm going back there and will once again give them too much to eat, until their bellies explode. I'll never be able to talk about even one percent of what I saw.

It's clear I'm not well, not well at all. It's not you who killed me, no, no, it's not even you. Be happy with Charlie. This really is my last letter.

J'ai ri.

And so Jerome David Salinger began imagining Holden Caulfield, who had already appeared in several of his published short stories ("Last Day of the Last Furlough," July 1944; "The Sandwich Has No Mayonnaise," October 1945; "The Stranger," December 1945; "I'm Crazy," December 1945; "Slight Rebellion off Madison," December 1946) and those refused by journals ("The Last and Best of the Peter Pans," 1942; "The Ocean Full of Bowling Balls," 1945), in which he pictures Holden Caulfield treated for mental problems in a psychiatric clinic after he had absconded to New York. And he began by writing this famous sentence: *"If you really want to hear about it, the first thing you'll probably want to know is where I was born and what my lousy childhood was like, and how my parents were occupied and all before they had me and all that David Copperfield kind of crap, but I don't feel like going into it, if you want to know the truth."*

In 1951, J.D. Salinger published *The Catcher in the Rye*. It is the despair of a Second World War veteran transplanted into the heart of a New York adolescent. The novel was refused by *The New Yorker* and the publisher Giroux (who also rejected Kerouac's *On the Road*). Finally accepted by Little, Brown and Company, it came out on July 16, 1951, at a price of three dollars. Salinger was respected in literary circles for his *New Yorker* stories: "A Perfect Day for Bananafish" (1948) and "For Esme—With Love and Squalor" (1950). *The Catcher in the Rye* was immediately hailed by Faulkner and Beckett. Jerry did no "promo."

"I can't explain what I mean. And even if I could, I'm not sure I'd feel like it," he said as a way of refusing all interviews.

What is the book's message? Either you conform to the

middle-class executive way of life or you end up in an asylum. Since 1951, the psychiatric hospital has been the horizon for free spirits in the capitalist system.

After three months, the book was number four on *The New York Times* Best Seller List, despite the newspaper panning it. Sixty years later, it still sells a million copies every year. This success and its consequences for society only have one equivalent in France: *Bonjour Tristesse,* by Françoise Sagan, published three years later.

11
THE TURNING POINT: 1952–1953

"Yes, our lives are merely strange dark interludes in the electrical display of God the Father!"

Eugene O'Neill, *Strange Interlude*, 1928

Chaplin's unpopularity in the United States became a daily problem for his family. In restaurants, people left their seats to call him a "Red" or "Bolshevik." Hollywood avoided Charlie and Oona. On New Year's Eve they scared off all the other stars. The failure of *Monsieur Verdoux* was a source of infinite sorrow for him. They felt increasingly detested, and not only by the Republicans. One day, somebody spat at Oona in the street. The feeling of aggression became palpable. Charlie twice refused to testify before the House Un-American Activities Committee. Depressed, he started writing a love story between a forgotten actor and a young dancer he saves from suicide. This would become *Limelight,* his last American film, a syrupy melodrama from which all the beauty of Chaplin's silent cinema had evaporated. He had predicted it himself: "If I talked

I would become like any other comedian." In the 1920s, Chaplin's great discovery was how to slow down the rhythm of burlesque, but this discovery only worked when there was no dialogue. People were drawn to his moving, drunk, flirtatious antihero, able to make us cry and laugh as he stole candy from babies or threw his cigarette over his shoulder before tapping it away with his boot. From the moment he started hammering us with grand, sententious speeches, he lost all his wonder and mystery. (The best thing about *Limelight* is Claire Bloom, who would later marry Philip Roth.)

The sense of a witch hunt in Los Angeles was so strong that Chaplin decided to organize *Limelight*'s premiere in London, in October 1952. He and Oona boarded the cruise liner with their four children (Geraldine, Michael, Josephine, and Victoria) to cross the Atlantic. J. Edgar Hoover, the FBI director, took that move as a spur to action. On board the *Queen Elizabeth,* they received a telex from the immigration service informing them that Mister Chaplin was forbidden to remain in the United States and would only receive an entry visa if he responded to charges of "moral turpitude and political unreliability" in front of the Immigration Department committee. At the same time, the American Justice Department announced the opening of an investigation into Chaplin. (Still today, all visitors to the United States are asked "Are you a Communist?" A positive response guarantees you long hours of interrogation.) All the newspapers carried headlines about Charlie Chaplin's "deportation." When he arrived first in London, then Paris, he was given a triumphant welcome. During a press conference at the Ritz on October 29, 1952, Chaplin declared that he would never return to America.

Like many wealthy people, Oona and Charlie chose to move to Switzerland, near Lake Geneva. The only problem was the Chaplins' entire fortune was in California. On November 17, 1952, with the greatest secrecy, Oona took charge of getting hold of the money. She took a plane from London to Los Angeles on the pretext of attending the United Artists board meeting. In reality, she hurried to Summit Drive to give notice to the staff and put the house up for sale, then headed to see Charlie's lawyer to instruct him to sell their shares. With her husband's power of attorney, she emptied all their safes at the Bank of America, taking possession of the original copies of Chaplin's films. She moved as many of their assets as she could by check and transfer into European accounts and withdrew the rest in thousand-dollar bills, which she stitched into the lining of her mink coat. Then she took a plane to London, during which she sweated heavily, refusing to take off the fur coat containing millions of dollars—the very scene filmed recently by Scorsese in *The Wolf of Wall Street*. The following year, Oona renounced her American citizenship and became a British subject. Chaplin would only return to Los Angeles once, in 1972, on an exceptional two-week visa, to collect an honorary Oscar, for which he would receive the longest standing ovation in the ceremony's history. I challenge anyone to watch that scene without the aid of several Kleenex.

At the beginning of 1953, the Sheraton Hotel in Boston looks like all the Sheratons of the time—the carpet is brown, the ceiling lights are silver, the lamps are orange. The walls are covered in geometric shapes, lozenges, and futurist rectangles. The receptionist's smile is so automatic that it bums you out. Doubt has no place at the Sheraton.

In his beige room, Eugene is trembling as he lies on his brown bed. He can no longer write. He congratulates Jerry on his short story collection that has just been published.

"I called because I wanted to see you. You were a friend of my daughter's. I'm going to die without seeing her again. I don't know how to forgive. I just can't do it. Neither can she. I wasn't made to be a father. Your book made me want to tell you that. I know you were her boyfriend before the old moppet. I... I never knew how to speak to Oona. I didn't even dare touch her arm. We never kissed each other in the family. I deserve to die alone, like my father.

It's so awful to have lost the ability to write when you don't know how to speak."

Eugene O'Neill pronounces these words as if reading from an invisible teleprompter, with the diction of an amateur actor, articulating too much and looking up at the ceiling. He has been preparing the speech for a long time it seems. His hand is trembling madly; he is drooling and he stinks. He is reciting this confession for himself. Perhaps he has confused Salinger with a priest and is hoping for absolution.

"Mister O'Neill," Jerry says after a long silence. "I understand you perfectly. You feel betrayed and you couldn't bear that she escaped you. The story ended for me a long time ago, but it's not too late for you to be reconciled with your daughter. Do you have her number in Switzerland?"

"Look what she sends me. Photos of my grandchildren. Her last letter is under my pillow, but I refuse to open it. Who am I to Oona, anyway? A bastard on his deathbed. I'll no doubt roast in hell, but I'll never see her again. Some failures are forever. There will be no reconciliation because we can't change the past, Jerome. Your book is very good because it's radical on this question. Your hero, Holden, is uncompromising. He can't stick hypocrisy. He is impolite and idealist.... He's a bit Irish like you, am I right? So you know that it's fucked. We've been separated for so long that a reconciliation this late wouldn't mean a thing."

"I don't understand why you called me here. To tell me that? I beg you to reach out to Oona before... Do you know what Buddha said when somebody spat on him?"

" ..."

"He said, 'I can't do anything with your insult. Take it back.'"

"Where do you live, J.D?"

"New York. Why?"

"Leave New York for a quiet house, far from society life. In your book you talk about a cabin in the woods…. Find it. Listen to the advice of an old schnook; it's in running away from their little living room schemes that you'll get to complete your work. I sense a madness in you at least as strong as mine…. The catcher in the rye: That's you during the war, right? Did you see a lot of your comrades die?"

"More than I could count, Sir. I see the survivors regularly. We never speak about the ones who stayed there. We drink and talk about baseball. The lists of names engraved on the monuments can hardly bring back the men they were. Some of them were real jerks, others were funny or yellow. Some of them would hit on the nurses or set their farts on fire! You refuse to talk to Oona and I'm unable to talk about those young guys who died in France and Germany."

"One day you'll see that you don't have the choice. They have to move out of your head one way or the other, and you'll finally be rid of them…. While you wait, leave New York. I promise you that's the best thing you can do."

"I came to beg you to call your daughter, and you want to banish me from Manhattan?"

"Exactly. That's my request. You're not going to refuse an old man his dying wish are you?"

A few weeks after this secret meeting, on November 27, 1953, in room 401 of the hotel, Eugene O'Neill died, murmuring: "I knew it. I knew it. Born in a hotel room and died in a hotel room."

Jerry moved to Cornish, and the Chaplins stayed in Corsier-sur-Vevey. His daughter wrote that Salinger had finished fifteen complete novels. My guess is that they all talk about the Glass family, a family destroyed by the war. One day we will know what this dead writer had to say about his dead friends.

Oona and Jerry would never see each other again. Officially.

Charlie Chaplin died on Christmas morning 1977 at the Manoir de Ban.
In their presents beneath the Christmas tree, his children found
a Super-8 projector and copies of some of his films from the 1910s.

12
OYSTER BAR,
SPRING 1980

"Men like me should never meet
women like you."

Guy de Maupassant, *Our Heart,* 1890

harlie Chaplin died on Christmas morning 1977 at the Manoir de Ban. In their presents beneath the Christmas tree, his children found a Super-8 projector and copies of some of his films from the 1910s. A wreck, Oona bought a duplex in New York on East 72nd Street, where she often went in order to flee the memories at Corsier-sur-Vevey. While there, she often saw Truman Capote. He picked her up from her place, wrapped up in a black cape and topped with a wide-brimmed hat. They went to Alcoholics Anonymous meetings together before finishing the evening at his apartment, at 870 U.N. Plaza (21st floor), listening to Xavier Cugat records. Oona was the only woman in the world still speaking to him after the *Answered Prayers* scandal. Oona was finding it difficult to live without Chaplin. The shanty Irish girl was drowning her grief in alcohol like one of Jean Rhys's heroines. In Corsier, she hid bottles in shoe boxes, drawers, under clothes, behind books, in

coat pockets, and even under her mattress. After her children left the manor, she almost became as misanthropic as
J.D. Salinger. Of course she saw the two other members of
the Golden Trio regularly—Carol (now married to the actor
Walter Matthau) and Gloria (known as Vanderbilt Cooper
since her fourth marriage). They spent occasional week-
ends in Malibu, remembering with a chuckle their nights at
the Stork Club, which no longer existed (the building was
demolished in 1966). From time to time, Oona rented a yacht
for a cruise in the sun, or hopped onto the Concorde on a
whim. When she was 54, she had a brief fling with an eager
young actor, Ryan O'Neal, 38, who had just filmed *Barry
Lyndon*. The following year, the painter Balthus invited her to
Rossinière to introduce her to David Bowie, who had come
to Montreux to record his latest album, *Heroes*. Sophia Loren
brought Michael Jackson to the Manoir de Ban after his con-
cert. Oona sold him the rights to "Smile" (which he massacred on one of his records) but refused to sell him the manor.
One evening at Carol's, Richard Avedon said to her:
    "They say you're unique…but I don't see it."
    "I'm not, you're right. Because everyone is."
    "Oh. Now I see it," said Avedon.

Most of the time, she didn't see anybody. Little by little,
Lady Oona O'Neill Chaplin forged a reputation as a reclusive
widow, a little nuts, who mixed vodka and antidepressants,
barefooted in her chauffeur-driven Rolls-Royce, until the
time when, one day in New York, in front of all her children
and grandchildren gathered around a birthday cake with sixty
candles, she proposed a toast in a heavy and uncertain voice:

"To you all, my dear family, on the occasion of my sixtieth birthday, I can finally say it: I hate my father, Eugene O'Neill!" before collapsing on the sofa with blood trickling from her nose.

In the seventies, Salinger sometimes went, very discreetly, to New York, London, or Paris. One day in 1980, Oona received a white calling card with these words written carefully in blue ink: "Dear Oona, don't ask me how I found your address in New York. I'll just remind you I once worked in counterespionage. I will be the tall fellow with gray hair, hiding behind a seafood platter and a bottle of chardonnay at the Oyster Bar in Grand Central Terminal next Monday at noon. Jerry." It took her a while to understand that it wasn't Jerry Lewis. She made the connection thanks to Grand Central, because Holden leaves his baggage there in *Catcher*. Oona lunched regularly at the Oyster Bar, drinking a great deal of champagne and ordering Santa Barbara stone crab claw with mustard mayonnaise. The waiters liked her because Lady Chaplin often left hundred-dollar tips.

That evening at home, Oona asked Truman Capote for

advice. Should she go? Capote could never stand Salinger: Socialites often confuse misanthropy with arrogance.

"So, you're really going to see the ex-soldier who writes like a baby?"

"Don't! You were lucky. You were too young to fight. You wouldn't have lasted ten minutes."

"Me? Surrounded by handsome boys in battle dress? *Chérie,* you're describing my wettest dream!"

"You're not funny. Just watching an execution traumatized you for life. Over there they saw hundreds of executions every day."

"*Pff!* Don't repeat this to anyone, but I think I wrote *In Cold Blood* just to beg forgiveness for not having gone to war. Ah! Pour me another vodka, babe. You know, sometimes I see Perry Smith [10] in the street. I know it's him. He follows me for a while, then he disappears."

"It's the same for me. When I'm drunk I think Charlie's

10. The murderer of the Clutter family, who was hanged in front of Truman Capote on April 14, 1965, at Lansing penitentiary, Kansas. He tells the story of this execution in the book *In Cold Blood.*

next to me. I start talking to him. I think of something that will make him laugh, and then suddenly I remember that he's dead, and he evaporates."

"Do you think we drink to forget or to remember?"

Pulling back the lavender-blue taffeta curtains, Truman looked out over the East River. The stripes on his seersucker suit matched the curtains. With his eyes wide open, he looked like Peter Lorre in *M*.

"No," Oona said. "I think we drink so that we can see them again."

"Do you realize that you are my only friend? You always have been. So go! Go see your catcher, but on one condition: Afterward you tell me everything at Studio 54!"

"54? I'd rather have my teeth pulled."

In one of his memoirs, Philippe Labro tells of how he ran into J.D. Salinger at Grand Central. Labro had approached a tall, stooped pensioner and asked, "Are you Mister Salinger?" The man just started screaming loudly: "*Aaaaahh!*" I don't know if the anecdote is true, but one thing is certain—I did well not to knock on his door in 2007. I wouldn't have appreciated Salinger yelling at me like a madman.

When Oona went into the restaurant, she didn't recognize him at first. Forty years had passed since they'd last seen each other, and Salinger wasn't the kind of guy to raise his arm so you'd notice him. But then she spotted an old skinny fellow with white hair, staring at her with his dark eyes. Everything had changed except his kindly eagle eyes. Gus Van Sant nailed it when he made Sean Connery play the role in *Finding Forrester*. The resemblance is striking. You could say he looked like a retired James Bond.

"You haven't changed at all," Jerry said. "I knew you at once. The prominent cheekbones, the facial bone structure. That's the secret. The structure never moves. Wrinkles don't change a thing. And you stayed slim."

"Don't be ridiculous! I had eight children. Stop razzing me. This hasn't started well. Waiter! A vodka please. Aren't you drinking?"

She nervously fondled her pearl necklace. She felt stupid for having put on a Chanel suit. She looked like a stuck-up old bourgeoise. Oona realized that it was the first time since Charlie's death that she had worried about someone else's opinion of how she looked.

"Chaplin was smart to have eight kids with you," Jerry said. "After that you were stuck with him in his Swiss castle."

"With you I would have been stuck in a cabin lost in the woods. I think that's worse!"

"He swallowed you up. Forced you to drop your acting career."

"Lighten up, Jerry! I was happy, not eaten up by ambition like you."

"You could have been a great movie star."

"Big deal! Today I'd just be an ex–movie star."

"You spent the best years of your life with a fogey in a wheelchair. He didn't! He lived with a young beauty! He never sacrificed anything for you!"

"Neither did I! I fell in love. Men are much more handsome at fifty than at twenty. I didn't sacrifice myself, and you know that well enough. You wrote it in one of your stories: There's nothing more interesting in this world than taking

*Oona lunched regularly at the Oyster Bar,
drinking a great deal of champagne. The waiters
liked Lady Chaplin because she often left
hundred-dollar tips.*

care of someone else. I was generous out of pure selfishness. And having children is great when you're depressive. It forbade me from killing myself like my brothers did."

Being with her again, Jerry remembered the pain he got in his gut every time he saw her. How could he have left for the war instead of staying with this chick? At the time he would have given his life for this old mare with ruddy cheeks and jutting teeth. He hated that he could no longer feel the burning passion like when he was twenty, but he was happy to still suffer all the same. Oona had always caused him marvelous suffering. Some people are born to do that. We grant them the right to torture us throughout our lives. It wasn't the pain he missed, but his youth. He was mad at her for having aged as much as he had. They were two ex-lovers with their lives behind them, their children, their memories, two old fogies sitting on iron stools, with only two things in front of them — a bottle of wine in an ice bucket (which they hadn't touched) and inevitable death, in ten years for her, thirty for him.

"You know," Jerry said, "I copied Chaplin. When I was fifty-four I got together with an eighteen-year-old kid. It lasted a year. Fortunately we didn't have children. She was called Joyce Maynard."

"So you see well enough, it's got nothing to do with age."

"Yes it does. The age gap is the secret of lasting relationships. I understood Chaplin after I started living like him. Youth, innocence, enthusiasm, and purity all at once... a new body and a confident soul. That's all an old guy needs."

"Before the war, you weren't a man. And I needed a man."

"A father, you mean."

"We were so young.... Charlie made me laugh. You only

made me sad. Listen, maybe this was a bad idea, let's leave it where..."

Instead of finishing this sentence, Oona preferred to finish her drink in one nonchalant gesture, as if to chase away bad thoughts through the ingestion of an 80-proof Russian spirit. To any of my dear pubescent readers, if you have stayed with me this far, know that this method never works. When her throat had stopped burning, she started speaking again, a little louder, to drown out the brouhaha of the other patrons clumped together around the bar.

"In 1941, you were unbearable, like all rascals your age. And you were much too tall. At least Charlie was the same height as me. We were perfectly proportioned."

"A Lilliputian family!"

"Jerry, I'm going to tell you one thing about Charlie. He was jealous, stingy, self-absorbed, fanatical, narcissistic, megalomaniacal, unbearable, cantankerous, snobbish, and a womanizer. But I loved him. What can I say? I loved him. I didn't choose him from a menu."

Salinger gulped down an oyster, making the sound of a bath as it drains.

"Charlie Chaplin was, without a doubt, the greatest satirist of all time," he went on, after wiping his mouth with a napkin. "And that's the very reason I have hated him all my life."

"I can't bear the fact he's gone. Honestly, it's appalling. I can't handle it, even with eight children I love. Living without him... Now, I'm against the age gap. I would give anything for one more minute with him sick, doddering, amnesic, and deaf. I'm suffering too much. Order me another

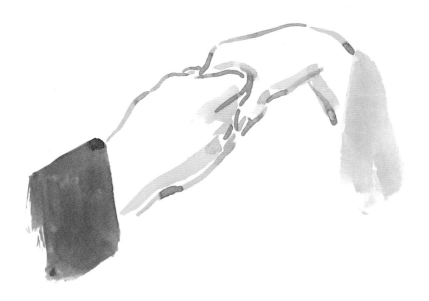

straight vodka, please. I'm too ashamed."

Jerry looked at the untouched bottle of white wine, then gestured to the waiter.

"While we're baring our souls," Oona said. "I always wondered why you never tried to sleep with me."

"You didn't move in bed, didn't say a word, you let yourself be fondled while clenching your teeth. Your feet were so cold.... You were so stuck up, so beautiful, but my God, what a tease!"

"I was shy, you dope! I was waiting for you to make the first move."

"It was true that we were young and stupid. In the army I fell in love with you because you were far away. I loved you because we never slept together and I was going to die the following day. I came here to tell you something about your husband. I really regretted sending that idiotic letter after your wedding. Chaplin might have escaped two wars, but he wasn't useless. He directed *The Great Dictator.* America was dragging its feet. Public opinion didn't want a war. There were too many bodies in 1918. The success of his film changed things. When I think how those bastards sent him into exile just because he was a militant for the Second Front. He was right: We should have gone into Europe one year earlier. Hey, I brought you a present."

Jerry leaned over, opened his travel bag, and took out a dish towel, folded in four. He set it down carefully on the table.

"What's that bundle of dirty washing?" Oona asked.

"Something that belongs to you. It's not in a great state, but you'll be able to fix it with a little superglue."

Oona unfolded the four corners of the cloth. On the table, in front of her, there were five pieces of white china, gleaming like egg white.

"A few bits are missing. Careful you don't cut your fingers."

Gently, with infinite care, Oona took the pieces and tried to reassemble them, like a child concentrating on a puzzle. She was able to reconstitute the silhouette of a stork, wearing a top hat and smoking a cigarette. Suddenly, she looked forty years younger, and her eyes shone with joy like a child on Christmas morning. Jerry got up. He was standing. He was leaving too quickly—it was a compulsion for him.

"Careful with the ash. It could be the remains of bodies burned at Dachau...or from Ernest Hemingway's cigar. I don't remember anymore. I never washed that thing. It was in a case dating back to the war. My daughter found it in the attic when she was tidying the house."

"You wrote me to return it? You're as mischievous as ever."

"I was happy to see you again. You're still perfectly perfect, Lady Chaplin."

"This ashtray really is all beat up. God, the Stork... How far away that all seems."

"I died in 1945, but you've been dead from the start. Ever since your father left you."

Oona avoided his gaze. Her hands were trembling, but Jerry was even more moved than she was. That was why he wanted to leave first, before he did something ridiculous. They turned their eyes to the glass ceiling at the same time.

"No, I beat my father: I lived."

"I shouldn't tell you this, but...I met Gene, just before he died. In Boston. A funny guy, your dad. He sent me a strange letter after *Nine Stories* was published. A kind of summons, like the one I sent you. He kept your letters under his pillow, you know. Poor old guy. You look like him. But he was much more alone than you are. See you soon, Glamour Girl of the Year," Jerry said, his voice quavering. "I have to go or I'll miss my train. Take care of yourself."

"Fine, go, you bloody little catcher. Go back to your hideout. Thanks for the stork."

"And you go back to your Swiss manor. There's nothing for you here. Go home and do what I do: meditate. Don't see anybody who isn't absolutely indispensable to you. Save yourself, in every sense. Adieu, little Oona. I'll let you pick up the tab, as usual."

Jerry kissed her hand. She pulled it back quickly so that he didn't see the brown stains on it. Oona lifted her glass; Jerry bowed like a Hindu. She took a bundle of dollar bills from her handbag. Seeing him smile, she realized that she had hardly ever seen him do that before. She waited until he was right at the other side of the station before letting herself go:

"Oh, shoot!"

Seeing her break down, the barman hurried over to ask what was wrong. His pity irritated Oona. She pulled herself together, dried her eyes with the back of the hand Jerry just kissed, finished her drink, and then the bottle. As she left the station, she put her sunglasses back on and the cool wind dried her cheeks. A few feet away, on the back seat of the Cadillac, she started crying again. Her impervious driver handed her the box of Kleenex without turning around. However, in his rearview mirror, he could see Oona stroking some pieces of broken china.

"To the Stork Club, please," she said.

A quarter of an hour later, the black limousine stopped in front of a public garden. The driver got out of the car and opened Oona's door. She climbed out with dignity. She stopped in front of a panel that said PALEY PARK: a tiny green space, squeezed in between two buildings on 53rd Street. Then she walked slowly toward the wall of water, to the back on the left, under the bushes, and took the pieces of the broken ashtray from her bag. By the corner of the wall, at the exact spot that table six once stood, she kneeled on the ground and started digging the earth with her hands, before burying the broken china in the flowerbed. Passersby, hurrying along, looked at her for a moment and wondered why this old bum was dressed in Chanel. Oona cried a little more as she climbed back into the Cadillac, and her driver told himself that this time, clearly, Lady Chaplin had completely lost her mind.

BIBLIOGRAPHY

Kenneth Anger, *Hollywood Babylon*

Antony Beevor, *The Second World War*

Truman Capote, *Answered Prayers*

Charles Chaplin, *My Autobiography*

Nicholas Foulkes, *High Society: The History of America's Upper Class*

Charles Glass, *Americans in Paris: Life and Death Under Nazi Occupation 1940–44*

Charles Glass, *Deserter: The Last Untold Story of the Second World War*

Ian Hamilton, *In Search of J.D. Salinger*

Raul Hilberg, *The Destruction of the European Jews*

Ghyslain Lévy, *Eugene O'Neill ou l'inconvenance de vivre*

Joyce Maynard, *At Home in the World: A Memoir*

Bertrand Meyer-Stabley, *Oona Chaplin*

George Plimpton, *Truman Capote*

Mary Louise Roberts, *What Soldiers Do: Sex and the American GI in World War II France*

David Robinson, Chaplin: *His Life and Art*

Shane Salerno and David Shields, *Salinger*

Margaret Salinger, *Dream Catcher: A Memoir*

Adam Saroyan, *Trio: Oona Chaplin, Carol Matthau, Gloria Vanderbilt—Portrait of an Intimate Friendship*

Jane Scovell, *Oona: Living in the Shadows*

Kenneth Slawenski, *J.D. Salinger: A Life*

J.D. Salinger left just one novel and about forty short stories and novellas, only thirteen of which were published in book form—nine in *Nine Stories*, two in *Franny and Zooey*, and two in *Raise High the Roof Beam, Carpenters, and Seymour: An Introduction*. Here is the list of other stories published before *The Catcher in the Rye*:

"The Young Folks," *Story*, March 1940
"Go See Eddie," *The Kansas City Review*, December 1940
"The Hang of It," *Collier's*, July 1941
"The Heart of a Broken Story," *Esquire*, September 1941
"The Long Debut of Lois Taggett," *Story*, September 1942
"Personal Notes of an Infantryman," *Collier's*, December 1942
"The Varioni Brothers," *The Saturday Evening Post*, July 1943
"Both Parties Concerned," *The Saturday Evening Post*, February 1944
"Soft-Boiled Sergeant," *The Saturday Evening Post*, April 1944
"Last Day of the Last Furlough," *The Saturday Evening Post*, July 1944
"Once a Week Won't Kill You," *Story*, November 1944
"A Boy in France," *The Saturday Evening Post*, March 1945
"Elaine," *Story*, March 1945
"This Sandwich Has No Mayonnaise," *Esquire*, October 1945
"The Stranger," *Collier's*, December 1945
"I'm Crazy," *Collier's*, December 1945
"Slight Rebellion Off Madison," *The New Yorker*, December 1946
"A Young Girl in 1941 With No Waist at All," *Mademoiselle*, May 1947
"The Inverted Forest," *Cosmopolitan*, December 1947
"A Girl I Knew," *Good Housekeeping*, February 1948
"Blue Melody," *Cosmopolitan*, September 1948

These short stories have never been republished, not in the U.S. nor anywhere else in the world, except on a Hungarian Web site, where I unearthed them. To date, the Salinger estate, comprising his widow Colleen O'Neill Salinger, his son Matthew, and his agent Phyllis Westberg, have prohibited posthumous publication of these classics of twentieth-century American literature.

ACKNOWLEDGMENTS

Frédéric Beigbeder and Assouline Publishing wish to thank the following for their valuable contributions to this work: Rafael Alterio, Adam Biles, Cheryl Della Pietra, Jay McInerney, Karin Nelson, Glenn O'Brien, Richard David Story, and Carl Swanson.